# SHADOWS
## IN THE SKY

# PETE CROSS

# SHADOWS IN THE SKY

WITH ILLUSTRATIONS BY COLIN STIMPSON

First published in Great Britain in 2007 by

**studio cactus ltd**

13 SOUTHGATE STREET  WINCHESTER  HAMPSHIRE  SO23 9DZ
TEL +44 (0)1962 878600  E-MAIL MAIL@STUDIOCACTUS.CO.UK

Printed in Great Britain by Short Run Press

For Dolly

# CONTENTS

# PROLOGUE
## 1973

*A* YOUNG WOMAN WAS driving a blue estate car steadily along the coast road. She marvelled at the colour-splurged hedgerows of late spring wildflowers flashing past, the blurred magenta streaks of red campion mingling with towering stalks of brilliant white cow parsley. Every now and then when an occasional gateway allowed her a glimpse through a hedge, she would catch sight of the rolling cliff tops, rough and untamed, with great masses of furze, heather and bramble. It looked a truly wild place. In the distance, where the cliffs rolled away out of sight, there was the great Atlantic, a blue so incredibly deep that she couldn't quite believe it was real.

Eventually the woman pulled up in a lay-by, turned the engine off and got out. The sun was dazzling, and the wind hit her full in the face. Quickly, she opened the car's back doors and put her coat on, then struggled to lift an unwieldy collapsed wheelchair out. She then knocked it into shape and hastily wheeled it round to the passenger door.

"Got your coat done up, Grandad?"

"'ess. All bundled up!" came the muffled reply.

The young woman helped the old man into the chair, shut the car door, and then pushed him over to a good spot. The wind buffeted their faces, and the smell of the sea was almost overwhelming.

"Wow," said the young woman. "What a view."

"'ess. Wow," echoed the old man, busily adjusting his binoculars.

"So is this where it's supposed to be then? The last one?"

"Somewhere along 'ere. Reckon 'e'll be along dreckly. I'll 'ang on 'ere as long as I can stand it, if 'is all right with you."

"Take as long as you like. We've come all this way, we'd better see it!" The young woman poured them both a cup of coffee from a flask and carefully tucked in the yellow-and-black tartan rug around her grandfather's knees.

"Don't you get cold now," she said. Then they waited.

"There he is!" shouted the young woman, pointing. The old man sniffed, gave his big red nose a wipe and peered through his binoculars.

"Nah, 'tis just ol' craw," he said. "You'm tell from the voice. 'tis a high pitched sorta 'cheow' sound they make. 'tis very distinctive, like." Birds wheeled and swooped all around them. All kinds of birds. An hour or so went by.

Another car drew up, a bigger, shinier one, and a middle-aged man got out. He was very well equipped for the conditions, fully insulated in wax jacket and waterproof leggings, topped off with a woolly hat. On his feet were stout walking boots.

"This the best spot for chough?" he called out cheerfully.

"Reckon so," replied the old man, "'e's s'posed to come this way to roost, so they say."

"Gosh," said the wax jacket man, "wouldn't it be fantastic to see him? The very last one in the country?"

"Wouldn't it just," said the young woman.

"I expect you remember seeing them when there were more about, sir," the wax jacket said to the old man.

"I don't ever remember more than a 'andful, not ever."

"But you are from around here, yes?"

"Oh 'ess. I'm from round 'ere," replied the old man, quietly, and carried on scanning the cliffs with his binoculars.

Half an hour went by. Still with his binoculars pressed to his eyes, the old man said, out of the blue, "I used to 'ave one fer a pet you know. When I was a lil' tacker."

"I say, really?" replied the wax jacket.

"Kept 'im indoors, trained 'im to eat out of me 'and. Lil beauty 'e was."

"Wasn't that a bit, well, cruel? I mean, isn't that partly why they've all gone now? You know, trapping, persecution, and suchlike?"

"Mmm, 'twas cruel. Did'n seem so bad at the time, though."

"What happened to it?"

"Let 'im go, in the end."

"Ah, that's good. So why are you here now, if you don't mind me asking?"

"Just wanna see one before I go. Sorta say goodbye," the old man sighed and removed the binoculars from his face, resting them on his blanketed knees. He continued to scan the landscape for any sign of the elusive bird. The wax jacket didn't reply. He didn't know quite what to say. Instead he found himself staring at the old man's face. The harsh sun illuminated countless blotches and scars, and the bitter wind had screwed up his face to betray every wrinkle. It was a face that you just knew had lived through hard times. In particular the wax jacket noticed the old man's right ear, which had a cloven lobe. There was a long upside-V shape where it should have been connected to itself, and it just hung down, quivering in the wind. The wax jacket found himself wondering how it got like that. In a fight? Some farming accident? He didn't like to ask.

And then an extra-strong gust forced the wax jacket to blink and he remembered with a start why they were all there.

"So when did you last see a chough, then?" he asked.

"I dunnaw, thirty odd year ago maybe, durin' the war," said the old man, wistfully. "There was still two or three about then, I reckon. We didn' call 'em 'chough' back then, though. They was always 'chows', 'cos of the noise they made I s'pose." And just then they heard it. An unmistakable, piercing 'cheow' sound, not far off.

"There 'tis!" whispered the old man urgently,

and spotted through all the crows and jackdaws the sight of the lone black bird. He pointed to help the others. The young woman and the wax jacket raised their binoculars and caught sight of it too. It swooped and ducked along the cliffs, and then passed by the birdwatchers so close that they had to lower the binoculars from their eyes. As it passed, it gave the loudest "cheow!" The three people stared, their mouths open.

"Fantastic," said the young woman, "I had no idea they were so beautiful. Look at the red bits! I can really see what all the fuss is about."

"And they really do think this is the last one, ever, don't they?" said the wax jacket.

"Oh 'ess, there ent no more left now. And this ol' feller's not got long left. 'is missus died five years ago, so I reckon 'e ent got much longer."

"What a dreadful story it is," said the young woman. The three people watched as the lonely chow swooped straight into a cave, disappearing out of sight.

"Well, I guess I'm done. Nice to meet you two. Bye," said the wax jacket, and went back to his car. The old man didn't hear him. His binoculars were pressed to his eyes. After a couple of minutes he finally lowered them. The young woman noticed his hands were trembling. He stared at the place where the chow had been, his eyes narrowed to slits against the powerful wind.

"Come on Grandad, we'd better get going," said the young woman, her face quite red from the wind and sun. "I'm sure you're colder than you're letting on." She helped him back into the car, put his wheelchair in the back, and drove off back the way they'd come.

A few minutes later, the lonely old chow reappeared from the cave, and landed lightly on the flat top of a huge pointed rock, which was all covered in yellow lichen. The rock was just below the lay-by where the cars had parked. He carefully preened for a few minutes, taking his time. He was slightly lame in his left leg. A group of gulls flew past him, a couple of them making a half-hearted attempt to dive-bomb him, then continuing on their way. The chow didn't flinch. He'd seen it all before. That old, lonely chow, whose wings didn't carry him as swiftly any more, looked as if he was just waiting for his time to come. He flapped his achey old wings a couple of times and took off, swooping and dipping his way back along the cliffs.

He had one last journey to make, one final job to do. It was going to require all the strength his tired old body could muster, but if he could reach his destination then all was not lost.

BOOK I

# Yowynk

## 1700

# The Stinky Cave

Many, many years ago, battered by the waves of the Atlantic Ocean, there stood a huge cliff. It was so tall that if you stood your house right next to it, and put two more just like it on top, they still wouldn't be as tall. Nowhere near. It was a mighty cliff.

The best bits about it were the crags and crevices. All the years of being hammered and lashed by the winds, and the Atlantic, and the rain, had created great dark holes and gullies in the cliff. Some of them were so deep and dark you could even call them caves. And it's one particular cave that we're interested in.

A person couldn't look into this cave, because there was no way of getting to it. You might be able to look into it if you had a really big boat, but it would have to be really big, or you'd be dashed on the rocks by the thundering waves. And if the boat was that big, then you wouldn't be able to get close to the cliffs anyway, so you'd have to look into the cave with binoculars, so, well, you might as well not bother. The floor of the cave was all shingly stones, which would tumble and roll when the waves took them, and sometimes, when the big winter swells came, the sound of the shingle in the cave would be quite deafening. They would be thrown in and out along the cave's floor with such force that they would all roll as one, like a giant pebbly wave. And sometimes, when the storms raged out over the great Atlantic Ocean, the unusually strong currents would rip great slimy heaps of seaweed from their home and drape them all over the floor of the cave. Piles of black, blistery bladderwrack, and huge ribbons of smooth, slippery kelp would be heaped so deep that it would come up to your waist if you stood in it. When the moon was only half full and the tides had no power to them, then sometimes the sea wouldn't come in far enough to reclaim the beach twice a day, and the dank seaweed would sit there and rot. The whole cave would stink so badly sometimes that you or I probably couldn't stand it. But eventually the tide would come in high enough to whisk it all back out again, and it would be gone in one go.

Now, you might be getting the impression that

the cave wasn't a very nice place to be. But there were certain creatures who loved it in there. For them it was just about perfect. For them there was no better place to be. The noise, the darkness, the occasional stinkiness, well, that was just how they liked it. The walls of the cave were made up of nooks and crannies, cracks, shelves and ledges. Nothing was smooth on the walls of that cave. But there was still plenty going on. Way up in the darkness, above the noisy shingly stones, and the stinky seaweed, high up on a ledge, there was a nest. A bird's nest. And in the nest, there were four little white eggs, speckled with brown, and all clustered together.

The nest, and the eggs, belonged to two chows. Two beautiful, red-beaked, red-legged chows, who'd decided that this was quite the best spot to build their nest, and had then spent weeks collecting all the bits of dried seaweed and sticks and roots to make a perfect framework, followed by the softer stuff for its lining. They'd used anything they could find, as long as it felt right; wispy grass, and the dried flower heads of the wild carrot. Bits of heather and prickly sprigs from the furzey bushes. Softest of all was the moss, and the thistledown, and the oily grey sheep's wool they'd find caught in amongst the brambles and the hawthorn. And of course there were feathers in there too, because there were always plenty of those about. They used anything to make it soft so the fragile eggs wouldn't roll about and break. Altogether, they'd made a very suitable home for their precious clutch of little speckled eggs, which were as safe as they could be in that fine nest, high up on that rocky ledge, on the wall of that dark, dark cave, in the middle of that mighty cliff, battered by the Atlantic Ocean.

# Hungry

The four little speckled eggs were twitching and making tiny tapping noises. Over the next few days all four hatched, bursting open to reveal four baby chow chicks. Now it must be said that although the chow is about the most beautiful bird around, the chick doesn't look too special. It's almost bald, and sort of bulgy looking, with closed eyes, and funny little stumpy wings that look like nothing more than flaps of skin. And it just sits there all day, sticking its ugly gaping beak in the air whenever it gets a sniff of food. But the mother and father, they didn't care much about this. No animal cares much about whether its baby is cute or not. It just wants to look after it, simple as that. The father chow was quite tired already, having spent the last three weeks feeding his mate, who'd been busy sitting on the little speckled eggs. But now the real work was beginning for both of them, as those chicks were going to need feeding as often as possible for the next month or so. I wouldn't want that kind of responsibility. But animals just get on with it, and so did the mother and father chow.

They would emerge from the cave at dawn, and work harder than they had ever worked to find enough food for four hungry little chows. They couldn't fly too far away, even though that's where some of the choicest creepy-crawlies were, because they had to stay close to the nest. So they'd try extra hard to find whatever they could in all the special places they knew within a ten-minute flight of the nest. The only pause in their busy food-finding day would be a few minutes here and there to preen. Keeping your feathers all clean and tidy is a very important responsibility for a chow, so they'd always make time during the day to find a nice bare rock where they could keep an eye out for trouble. Here they'd perch together in the sun and run each feather carefully through their long scarlet beaks, removing any nasty bits of dirt that had no business being there.

There were two little male chow chicks in the nest and two females. They sat in their nest, in the almost pitch-dark cave, unaware of the world outside. They could see light, out there somewhere, but had no idea what it was. They didn't know much about much. Babies never do. But there's one thing they did very well. They started growing. Day after day they sat there, waiting for their mother and father to return with their slimy, wriggly dinner. And breakfast, and supper. And every meal in between. The parents would swallow it when they caught it, and then cough it up again for the chicks. Pretty revolting to us, but pretty tasty to a chick, and that's all that matters. Weeks went by, and the nestlings grew proper feathers, and began to flap their little wings, and look all around them, and notice what their parents were doing. Their parents were busy all the time. When they weren't foraging to find food, they were flying. When they weren't flying, they were preening, or feeding the chicks. When they weren't feeding the chicks, they were patching up the nest, and generally keeping things spick and span.

And then something awful happened. One of the girl chicks, in an over-excited moment of wing-flapping, got a bit carried away. She was already sitting very close to the edge of the nest, and her parents were away finding food, so they weren't there to nudge her back in. She lent over at the wrong moment, then tried to regain her balance, but it was too late. She tumbled out of the nest, down, down into the darkness. No chow ever saw her again. When their parents returned with food, the three remaining nestlings made even more noise than usual, but the parents knew that there was no time to be sad about such a loss. They knew exactly what had occured, and simply carried on with the job of feeding their young ones. Not everything can survive in the wild, and sometimes these things happen. At least the three surviving chows could have more to eat now, because there was just the three of them. And so they would grow stronger as a result. They certainly took more care in the nest from then on.

# The Bouncy Green Stuff

Now the young birds looked like proper little adults. They'd watched their parents swoop in and swoop out again hundreds of times, and deep within them they knew that they were going to do this too. Or die trying. To encourage the nestlings to leave the nest, their parents would cry out to them from outside the cave. The first chick to go was one of the two boy chows, who we'll call Yowynk, even though the chows didn't really have their own names, because they were birds. Yowynk had spent days standing up, and flapping, and stretching, and practising. He didn't quite know why, but something grew so strong in him, an urge so overpowering that he cared more about leaving the nest than he did about staying. With a scream he stretched his wings to their full span, and leapt from the nest. What a feeling! He wobbled, mid air, from side to side, adjusted himself and swept upwards, and headed generally in the direction that his parents had always flown – towards the daylight. Suddenly his whole world was blindingly bright. Squinting against the sun, trying to head towards his parents' calls, he managed to land in a heap on a large rock, just a little above where his parents had positioned themselves. He could still hear them calling, and became aware that they were just a couple of hops away. They both called out again. Yowynk stretched out his wings for balance, and jumped down to land right next to them.

Now Yowynk looked around him. This new world was incredible. It was a world of vastness, of colours, of life. There were a thousand blues and greens, browns and greys. There was wetness, and breezes, and strange, unfamiliar smells. And, most of all, there was light. The light was almost unbearable. He didn't even know what light was, let alone all this other stuff! It was a world he'd had no idea existed. It was terrifying, and fascinating, and exhilarating. But it felt good. Above the cliffs he could make out that the land was all green, and some sort of huge, dark animals were there, noses to the ground, eating.

Most amazing were the birds. Yowynk had only ever really been aware of his brother and sisters in the nest, and his two parents. But now, as he looked about him, he saw huge white birds, and gawky black birds with scrawny necks, and smaller white birds soaring above. Best of all, there were chows. They were all over the place; dotted about on the rocks, squabbling, pecking at the ground in the distance. In the air above him, Yowynk could see chows doing amazing things, soaring, tumbling, travelling at incredible speeds. It was all too much. He looked at his parents, then he looked back at the cave that had been his home his whole life, and let out a little "cheow!" But he didn't want to go back there. He liked it out here, the new place. His father brought Yowynk a helping of insects, which he took comfort in and swallowed greedily, and he was soon joined by his brave younger sister, who we'll call Lowen. Their brother Hogh had a little more trouble saying goodbye to his comfy nest, and was reluctant to leave the dark familiarity of the cave. Hogh flew from the nest to a nearby narrow ledge within the cave and stayed there for quite some time, regardless of the encouraging calls of his family. Eventually he jumped to another ledge, and then back to the first. But by the end of the day his instincts were too much for him, and Hogh joined the rest of his family out in the light.

All animals communicate with each other, in some way. Because we are humans, and only understand our own languages, we don't have much of an idea what other animals are talking about. Chows, for example, sound like they are just screaming 'Cheeow!' all the time. After all, that's how they got their name. But this simple sound can actually mean a lot of things, if you're a chow. It just depends on how the chow 'cheows' it. When the fledglings had first found their voices, all they could yell was 'Meeee!' and 'Food!' A fairly limited repertoire. But now they were learning fast, as only young things can. And this was just as well, because their mother and father had an awful lot to teach their young family.

"Stay close," cheowed their father, "and you'll be safe."

Yowynk understood his father, but during the next few days found it awfully hard to remember to stay near his family, when he'd much rather have been out testing his flying skills. Fortunately, Yowynk's strongest instinct was to find food to fill his empty belly. He was hungry all the time, especially now that he was getting so much exercise instead of just sitting in his nest, yelling. His parents knew what they were doing. They knew that if they fed their fledglings less and less, they'd start feeding themselves. And so the three little chows watched everything their parents did, and copied them in every action. Their young beaks were shorter and still quite dull compared with the beautiful scarlet beaks of their parents. But they started to find small ants and the odd beetle, and these tasted good, so they wanted more. Slowly, and carefully, the mother and father took the youngsters further afield.

After a few days, they knew it was time to take them onto the short grass way up on the mighty cliff's top. Things were very different up here. Instead of having to stick their beaks into any old rocky crevice in the hope of finding a solitary earwig, the chows could now probe deep into the soft soil, and find a far more appetising meal.

"It's much better up here!" cheowed Yowynk's

sister Lowen, excitedly jabbing into the lovely springy turf. "Can we stay here forever?"

"The bouncy green is always where the good stuff is," their mother replied. She showed them how to recognise an anthill from a distance, and how to catch the grasshoppers emerging from their eggs. Best of all, she showed them how to find the juicy leatherjackets, which are the grubs of the daddy-long-legs. You and I wouldn't know where to start, but a clever chow, with its long red beak, always knew where to look. Now that the days were long and warm, the leatherjackets were at their busiest feeding on the tiny tubers of certain plants underneath the soil. The chows recognised those plants from a distance, and therefore where the leatherjackets would be. They could recognise the plantain, and the thistle, and all the different types of grasses, and about a hundred more plants besides. They all meant something to a chow. Once they'd found a promising looking spot, Yowynk, Lowen and Hogh soon learned how to find the leatherjackets by pecking at the springy turf. They'd gouge, and prise, and hop from side to side to find the best angle, and if the grub didn't appear, they knew they had the wrong spot, and moved on. But if they did find one they squawked and squabbled and swallowed it as quickly as possible because they were hungry, hungry chows, and nothing in the world was as tasty to a young chow as a big, juicy leatherjacket grub.

"I found it! It's mine!" Yowynk shouted, struggling at the same time to turn it in his beak so that he could gulp it down.

"That's what you think! I'm bigger than you! I need it!" replied Hogh, snatching it and swallowing it whole. He wasn't really bigger. Just greedier. That night, roosting back in the stinky cave, Yowynk fell asleep with big fat leatherjackets dancing before his eyes.

And when he woke up, guess what the first thing he thought of was. His brother Hogh must have been thinking the same thing, because the first thing he screeched was, "Can we go back to the bouncy green stuff? I'm starving!"

"Yes, of course," replied their mother. "All the best food is there. But today we'll go to a different spot first, for a new lesson."

Hogh was worried that he wouldn't get enough

to eat, and quietly cheowed to Yowynk, "I hope it's not too far. I'm not sure if I can make it."

"You'll be all right," replied Yowynk. But he was really thinking "You greedy chow. We're all just as hungry." They flew straight to the spot they'd been to the day before, but they had barely touched down when their father took off and called, from a height, "Come on you lot! We've got something to show you!"

They flew for another two minutes further west along the coast, and landed on a small grassy area where many animals were grazing. The young chows were frightened at first, but their parents didn't seem at all concerned.

"Don't worry young ones, the big four-legs are our friends. They're not the ones you need to watch," cheowed their mother.

Sure enough, the sheep and ponies that were scattered all about them looked quite friendly, and they certainly didn't seem to mind a few chows about the place. The young ones' parents now set about teaching them exactly why the animals were their friends. It was actually their droppings that the chows were most interested in. Well, not

the droppings exactly, but what lay within them.
Yowynk, Lowen and Hogh soon learned that when
they pecked at them, they could be rewarded with
a real feast. But they had to be just right. There was
quite a knack to it. The dark green, fresh droppings
seemed to have plenty of tempting, juicy-looking
flies around them, but they'd all fly away when
the chows ventured anywhere near them. Besides,
when they tried to stab into the fresh dung, their
beaks would stick to it and they'd be in a fine mess.
They'd have to wipe it off on the springy turf, and
that didn't do any chow any good at all.

"Yeeuugh, it's all stuck to my beak!" Yowynk
exclaimed.

"You have to go for the older, dryer ones,"
cheowed his father, kindly. Sure enough, stabbing
through the crust of the older cowpats they found
all sorts of juicy delights. By the time a hungry
chow had finished with one, the crust would be
scattered all about the place. There were beetles
and centipedes, and different winged flies, and
grubs, and the occasional nest of tiny eggs. There
must have been up to a dozen different kinds of
meal within every cowpat, and the young chows

quickly learned to go straight for them whenever they spotted one.

They had great fun squabbling over the bounty that had been provided by the sheep, and ponies, and cows, and soon they weren't frightened of these animals at all. They quickly learned to enjoy their company.

"They really are our friends, aren't they?" cheowed Yowynk to Hogh. But Hogh couldn't answer, because his beak was full.

"Your belly will get you into trouble one day," warned Yowynk.

For several days the chows fed on the short, short grass, pecking and gouging at any likely looking areas that caught their fancy. But increasingly Yowynk and Lowen found themselves watching the sky. While their brother Hogh was busy looking for more to eat, the two of them were fascinated by what they saw going on above them. There were so many other chows about, and they were doing incredible things overhead. They'd fly past them at such a speed that they looked as if they'd never stop, constantly twisting and dipping and swooping. And all the while they'd be cheowing to each other so joyously. Yowynk and Lowen wanted to be up there too. They couldn't wait.

There was a special rock just outside the stinky cave, the one that Yowynk had first landed on. It was a pointy shape, but had a nice flat top, and was covered in yellow lichen, which felt good under the young chows' claws. The pointy rock was the perfect place for an early morning preen, and on a bright day, when the sun reached its highest point in the sky, it would hit the rock and bathe it in sunshine. The chows liked it when this happened. The feeling of the sun on their black feathers in the afternoon was lovely, and several times a day, if the sun was out, they'd stop here for a while. One afternoon, Yowynk, Lowen and their father found themselves on the pointy rock together.

"When can we fly properly, father?" asked Lowen. "You know, really soar, like we've seen the other chows do?"

"You can't soar before you've learned to flap," their father replied, in loud cheows.

But Yowynk and Lowen couldn't contain themselves. If you've ever watched a magpie, which is also a type of crow, you'll know how they love to strut. They strut with their great long legs, all perky and confident. Chows are the same. But when they get excited they like to bounce. They bounce sideways, in great bounds. They find they cover more ground this way, and, well, it just feels good. Yowynk's legs felt strong now, so as his father patiently tried to talk to them, Yowynk was impatiently hopping and bouncing from one side of the pointy rock to the other. Lowen did the same. Each of their great hops was getting bigger than the last, and it was driving their father crazy.

"When can we fly properly, though?" asked Lowen again.

"Stay still a minute, and don't you talk back to me," replied their father, trying to remain patient. He remembered the feeling too.

"But we want to soar, like we've seen you do, and all the other chows," Yowynk joined in, bouncing across the rock so far that he almost fell off. Then he bounced back the other way, and cheowed, "Why can't we?"

"Because there are dangers. So many dangers."

"Dangers? When can we hear about them?

When? When?" cheowed Lowen. With that, their
mother and Hogh landed on the pointy rock.

"We can start tomorrow," she replied.

# Danger

Next morning, the whole family were on the pointy rock, bright and early.

"Now," cheowed the father, "listen to me, because this is important." Of course, the young ones were all busily hopping about, and preening, and pecking at bits of lichen, because that's what chows do. But they were also listening very carefully.

"The reason we've always told you to stay close is because the world is full of great danger," he continued. "So far we have always been there to keep an eye on you. But the three of you are older now and must start to look out for yourselves."

"What must we look out for? What?" asked Yowynk, excitedly.

"You see the greedy white ones?" replied their mother.

"Which ones?" asked Lowen, looking at the different gulls that were all about them, flying, perching, squabbling amongst themselves.

"All of them. That means the small ones, the huge ones with the black backs, and worst of all them, the yellow-beaks." Yowynk looked as two of these yellow-beaks flew past, squawking.

"Always watch them, because they will kill you as soon as look at you," cheowed their father. The young chows jumped and cheowed anxiously at the thought.

"Why? How?" asked Yowynk.

"They'll mob you. They'll get you in the sky. They'll get you on the ground. They'll get you in your nest, whether you've hatched or if you're still in your egg. They'll sneak up whenever you're not looking, and they'll always be there, waiting. You must always be watching."

"But they look so clean, and they chat to us!" exclaimed Lowen.

"It means nothing," warned their mother. "They're filthy. I've seen them eat the foulest of things. They don't care. They have no morals, no pride, no dignity. Never go near one, or let one get near you."

"But they're good fliers too! I've seen them! They'll catch us!" screeched Hogh, with fear in his eyes.

"It's true they're good fliers, but we are better.

No bird flies like us. You'll see."

"So that's what all the fuss was about," thought Yowynk to himself later that morning as the family explored a new soft, grassy knoll. He was beginning to look upon those greedy white ones in a whole new light. They'd always come a bit close for comfort, chatting and squawking and teasing and taunting, and now he knew why. He wouldn't be going near any of those fellows again. But he watched them intently, from a distance. And he could see what his parents meant. Even when a chow was hungry, he couldn't just eat any old thing. But the greedy gulls ate anything and didn't care. A chow had to eat little and often, but the greedy gulls would binge on the foul entrails of fish flung into the air behind the fishing boats, eating huge amounts at a time if they were available. Then they'd just do nothing for the rest of the day, but sit around squabbling and being lazy. It was the same when they flew. The greedy gulls never seemed to work that hard. They'd just soar, riding the air currents as much as possible without having to do any wing work. Gulls were just plain lazy.

During the next few days Yowynk witnessed them eating rotting dead things in the sea, and even, on one occasion, devouring one another. Those greedy white ones made Yowynk nervous. A chow was altogether a more finely tuned machine. Like any intelligent, well-engineered piece of equipment, a chow had to have the right fuel. You couldn't expect to be the best flier around and live on fish guts.

# Flying

The youngsters were almost fully grown. Their beaks and legs were becoming redder all the time, their young bodies felt more agile in the air, and when the five of them flew together they looked like a real flock. Except with chows, a flock is called a chattering. There are special names for flocks of other birds too. A gaggle of geese. A charm of finches. We humans love to give names to things. A starling doesn't know we call it a starling, and a flock of starlings doesn't know we call it a murmuration of starlings, and I'm quite sure they couldn't care less. Some of these names are very strange indeed. An unkindness of ravens. A parliament of rooks. A murder of crows. An exaltation of larks. So a chattering of chows seems like as good a word as any. After all, it's better to be in a chattering than in a murder, isn't it?

Increasingly, Yowynk found that his own family chattering joined up with a larger chattering, making twenty or thirty in number. Yowynk, Lowen and Hogh became very aware of the presence of other chows. It felt good to be part of a community. They felt stronger. But at the end of the day, the family would always end up roosting separately from the others. The days were long now, as long as they ever are, and the short nights were warm and still. All day the chows would roam, swooping and diving, searching for good food spots.

"Big group of four-legs down there. You know what that means!" cheowed their father.

"Food!" cheowed Hogh, wasting no time at all.

Some days they would find themselves heading west for half an hour, until the young ones worried they'd never make it back home. But they soon realised that there were landmarks that were easy to recognise, and getting home was never a problem. With every day that passed, Yowynk saw more amazing things. He looked down on great towering structures of stone. They were like vast rocks, but square in shape. Some had tall plumes of smoke billowing from them, and made terrifying noises. Usually there were many animals around them, some pulling others, or gathered in large groups. And there were people, who were just another type of animal to a chow. Yowynk noticed that sometimes there were chows perching and roosting on some of the structures. They were always the crumbling-looking places with no people around them. But his parents warned the young birds not to go near any of them.

"The big two-legs are strange creatures indeed. Always fly away when you see one."

"Why?" asked Lowen.

"You don't ever want to find out," they replied.

As the young birds matured, their flying skills improved dramatically. Chows are amazing fliers. They have long, strong feathers on each wing called primaries, and six of these primaries make up the broad wing tip. They look like great black fingers, splaying out just as much as if you spread the fingers on your own hand out. These fingers are the key to their flying. "Look after your feathers, and they'll look after you," explained the young chows' father. And slowly they were taught the painstaking art of correct preening. They learned how to run their beautiful, black wing feathers through their beaks, one by one. If there were any old bits of dust or dirt, or nasty little parasites, or bits of old feathers, they'd be found, and got rid of. Those chows didn't miss a thing. At the same time, they would be spreading their special oil all over every feather, which helped keep them sleek and waterproof. Most importantly, this oil was the secret to how the chow was the blackest, shiniest bird around. Then they'd start on their smaller covert feathers, which they could manage a few at a time. By the end of every day, there would be no part of themselves that hadn't been checked. The young chows learned that the most important job of the day, apart from finding food, was to make time for preening.

Weeks passed, and then the long days slowly started shortening again. Yowynk began to notice that there were far fewer leatherjackets around. They'd all hatched into daddy-long-legs. So the chows had to concentrate on finding other insects. It was all part of the great circle of life, and Yowynk's parents explained that they would all be able to binge on their favourite leatherjackets again when the days grew longer.

Yowynk and Lowen didn't even realise it, but they were spending more time with the larger chattering than with their own family. Hogh was different; he was happy to fly along with his parents just as long as they led him straight to food. Yowynk and Lowen were enjoying the company of all the new chows they were meeting. Then suddenly they weren't even returning to the stinky cave to roost with their family. At the end of a day's exploring they ended up much further west along the coast with a chattering of thirteen other chows, settling in amongst some unfamiliar crags and ledges for the night. Back at the stinky cave, their brother Hogh missed them. He drifted into sleep feeling quite alone, wondering where his brother and sister had ended up. But next morning he thought little about it. All he was concerned about now was filling his belly. Their parents were quite happy that Yowynk and Lowen had flown the roost. Now they could relax a bit. They knew they'd done their job, and taught them well. There was just one thing niggling them. One thing they hadn't had time to teach them before they left.

# Black-cheeks

"We've never roosted away from our cave before," cheowed Yowynk quietly to a young female chow he found perched next to him and Lowen.

"We'll look out for you. We all have to look after each other," the chow replied. "There are a lot of older ones amongst us, and they know how to go about things. We're quite safe."

Lowen quietly cheowed, "Thank you."

Next day the sky was almost cloudless. Although the nights had a new chill to them, when the sun was out it was still nice and warm, and the chattering of chows looked spectacular in flight. You can always tell a chow by the way the fingers on its wingtips swoop upwards as it flies. A chow can step off a cliff top, catch an updraught and rise fifty metres in a couple of seconds, then with a slight adjustment, veer off at 90 degrees to the right, hold that position for as long as it likes, then, folding its wings back along its slender body, plummet vertically down like a gannet diving for fish. Then with another slight adjustment it will stall, hang motionless in the air and then skewer upwards again, travelling almost as fast in the opposite direction. If you thought a gull was a good flier, wait until you see a chow.

The most wonderful sight of all is a buoyant chattering of chows working their way along the cliff tops, dipping and swooping, fingers splayed out, wing tips flicked upwards, heads tilted this way, then that way, eyes calmly perusing the land below them for good food stops. All the while they're calling; "Cheoooow! Cheeeeeow!!" It's as if they are laughing with the sheer joy of it all, with the wonder of life. They fly exuberantly. You have to see it to believe it. Chows are birds in complete control of their world. I really can't imagine anything we humans could ever do that would come close to the feeling a bird gets when it jumps off a branch, or a rock, or a cliff top, spreads its wings and flies. And the most impressive thing of all is that chows look as if they aren't even trying.

Yowynk and Lowen felt ever so grown up, travelling with their new friends. Even though they covered great distances during the days, for the first week the chows returned to the same cliff to roost for the nights. Then the chattering began to move steadily along the coast by day, finding a new spot to roost each night. Yowynk and Lowen weren't really sure why they needed to travel so far, but it was exciting, and they saw little reason to leave the group. Certainly they were finding no shortage of food every day. One evening as they settled for the night, they overheard two of the other chows.

"It could be bad. I've smelled this sort of breeze before," cheowed one, in a hushed tone.

"We don't know yet. It's too soon to tell. We can just shelter here if it doesn't last too long," replied the other.

"What do they mean?" Lowen asked her brother.

"Don't know," Yowynk acted unconcerned. "Let's just wait and see. No point worrying."

Next morning the group was continuing west, riding the air currents as only a chow can do, looking out for the next promising-looking bit of ground. Slightly further out over the sea flew a pair of rock doves. Yowynk and Lowen were quite used to seeing these as they were common, and no threat. The doves weren't terribly good fliers, and made frantic clapping sounds with their wings whenever they took off, madly flapping to stay on course. They were always minding their own business, and never looked all that concerned about what was going on around them. As they passed the two doves Yowynk became aware of a small dot in the sky above them. It looked nothing more than a tiny black cross, way, way up. Suddenly the chattering of chows around Yowynk erupted with excitement.

"What's happening?" exclaimed Yowynk.

"Don't know!" replied Lowen.

The chows dipped and swooped wildly, all over the place. There was no order to it, no composure – not like a chattering of chows at all. Some started cheowing in a dreadful fashion unfamiliar to Yowynk. Hearing this, they all joined in, in panicky cheows. Yowynk caught the odd phrase: "Look out!" and "Keep moving!" and "Black…." At that moment, from above, the tiny speck became a missile. It dropped faster than anything Yowynk had ever seen, faster than any chow could ever dream of. In the blink of an eye it hit one of the doves. There was an explosion of feathers in the sky, and the missile, with the poor dove struggling in its talons, continued to drop, more slowly now, then level off, and disappear into the distance. The terrified chows quietened down, and Yowynk called to the nearest chow, "What was it!?"

"Black-cheeks!" he cheowed back. "Keep going!"

Chows aren't much good at chatting on the wing. Their amazing flying takes up all their concentration, so they limit their conversation to basic stuff just so they don't get into trouble. That's what we hear, that loud cheowing when they're flying. But it's when they land that they really communicate, more quietly. And now there was much to talk about. A good while later, and much further along the west cliffs, the chows all landed. The young ones all wanted to know what had happened.

"What was it? What killed that flappy clapper?" asked Yowynk.

"What was it?" implored Lowen, wide-eyed. One of the older female chows hopped over to them.

"Didn't your parents tell you about Black-cheeks?" enquired the older chow. "He is the king of the skies. Even a chow can't beat him. That flappy clapper didn't stand a chance."

"Then how can we stay away from him? How?" cheowed Cara, the young chow who'd been so welcoming on their first night away from home.

"You can't. If he wants you for a meal, he'll have you." Seeing the terrified look in the young chows' eyes, the older chow went on, "But you can avoid him. You'll never outfly Black-cheeks, but you can make sure he never gets into a position to catch you."

"How? How?" pleaded Lowen, still not happy.

"Simple. Keep looking up. Black-cheeks can only get you if he's got a run-up. Make sure he's never up there, and you'll be safe from him. If you ever see him, warn your friends and get away as quickly as possible."

"That's it?" asked Yowynk, "Then we'll be safe?"

"Yes. Don't worry young ones. You don't often see Black-cheeks. He's lethal, but he's scarce. This is only the second time I've ever seen him. And there's no-one else in the sky who can get near you."

The black-cheeked peregrine was truly an impressive creature. There was nothing faster in the skies, as long as he was doing a straight dive. It was worrying for the young chows. First the greedy gulls, and now this. There seemed to be so many creatures trying to get them, they could never really relax. Learning to be a chow was turning out to be quite hard work.

# The Great Atlantic Storm

The days were very short now, and there was a fresh wind coming straight in off the sea. It wasn't a cold wind, but it was growing stronger all the time, so Yowynk, Lowen and their thirteen new friends found themselves constantly buffeted in the air. They never seemed able to fly in the direction they wanted to go. As for feeding, it was hard work locating food when you could hardly stand up. They stayed close to each other, and that night found some sheltered rocks in which they nestled to roost.

"The storms are on their way," cheowed an older chow, as they huddled together for the night. "I've seen it once before. We may have to move inland."

"Inland? Why? Is there food there?" asked Yowynk.

"There's not a lot to eat, but at least we can find shelter there. We can't stay here when the storms come. It's not safe."

Lowen was wondering how their parents and Hogh were going to cope back in the stinky cave.

"Can we stick with you?" Cara asked the older chow eagerly. "If the storm gets too strong? Can we?"

"Of course," she replied, "but stay close."

The wind hammered at the cliff face all night, and heavy rain came with it. Beneath them the black sea boiled and foamed, and the terrifying waves smashed against the cliff wall so hard that the young chows worried they'd be swept away by their spray. The wind howled and whistled through the rocks on which they were roosting, making strange swirling pathways through the channels and gullies as if frantically searching for something. The young chows were glad when dawn came. Except that it didn't really seem like dawn. The sky was so black with rain that it hardly became light at all. When the brave chows took off to go about their daily routine of finding food, they were in for quite a shock. The rocks on which they'd roosted must have been more sheltered than they'd realised, because as soon as they rose above them, the full force of the gale hit them. The chow in front of Yowynk was lucky not to be dashed on the cliffs, such was the force of the wind that took him. The young chows had never experienced anything like this, and they knew instinctively that these were not conditions they could survive in. All fifteen chows in the chattering made it to the top of the cliff and attempted to fly over the scrubby, rocky area at the top, in order to get to the nearest short grassy field. But it was hopeless. The vicious crosswinds were battering them all over the place. They had no control at all.

"Inland!" Yowynk heard their older chow friend cry. Most of the chattering carried on fighting against the wind, but a handful broke away and headed as best they could away from the cliff top, and straight towards places they'd never normally have dreamed of going.

After some time the older chow spotted a deep valley in the distance, and made her way towards it as best she could. The others followed. They knew that the lower they flew, the better their chances of protection from the howling wind. Sure enough, as they dipped down into the valley, the wind diminished, and the chows could fly almost normally again. They landed clumsily in a clearing, surrounded by trees that now towered above them. There were four of them; Yowynk, Lowen, Cara and the older chow.

"This is a strange place!" cheowed Lowen. "Must we stay here?"

"No, there's little for us here. We must carry on if we are going to eat!" replied the older chow.

"Come on then!" cried Yowynk, launching himself into the air. "No point in wasting time!"

"You're a bold one, I'll say that for you!" cheowed the older chow to Yowynk, as all four of them carried on along the wooded valley, dipping and diving and searching for a place to eat. It was still raining hard, but they were very relieved to be away from the wind. A large flock of squawking gulls passed them, too close for comfort, and it was all the chows could do to avoid colliding with them.

"Bullies," muttered Yowynk.

They became aware of a track running along the bottom of the valley, and occasionally they would spot the big two-legs, and more of the strange big stone structures that they recognised from home.

The track looked promising; in places it was quite wide and the grass was short. They landed briefly, and managed to pick up a few earwigs and ants here and there, but there were more and more two-legs about, so they didn't stick around.

Still flying low, the chows now began to see big groupings of the stone structures, and more two-legs than the young ones had seen before in their entire lives.

"All these two-legs!" cheowed Lowen shakily. "It doesn't look safe!" Not only did they keep seeing the two-legs, but there were also more and more gulls about, squawking and fighting and generally making a nuisance of themselves.

"No, we must be careful. But there is food here, look." The older chow was right. Although this was a strange-looking world of two-legs, with countless stone structures, and smoke and noise, there were open areas of short, short grass, and hundreds of big four-legs about the place. So the chows landed and started feeding, finding plenty to eat in the cowpats, and in the crevices of the stony hedges.

That night the four chows roosted on a

dilapidated-looking wall. They hadn't noticed any two-legs in the area, so judged it to be as safe as anywhere. The young ones couldn't believe where they'd ended up, but they were determined to put on a brave face.

"It's exciting, isn't it?" cheowed Yowynk.

"Well, I suppose so," replied Cara.

"It's only until the storm is over. Then we can all go back to the coast," cheowed the older chow. "Don't worry, young ones, I've been here once before. We can survive here, if we're careful."

"Careful? Why? Because of the two-legs? Or the greedy white ones? Why do we need to be careful?" asked Lowen nervously.

"Let's sleep," replied the older chow quietly. "We'll see what tomorrow brings."

A part of Yowynk was actually loving all this. After all, it was quite an adventure. They'd left home, learned all about Black-cheeks, survived the worst of the storm, found a new place sheltered from the awful winds, and were now roosting with fairly full bellies. Things could be a lot worse. But Yowynk had no idea what the next day held in store for him. The next day, poor Yowynk was to suffer the fright of his life.

* * *

The chows were out looking for food the following morning when it was barely light at all. They sensed they needed to make the most of their time, and so they didn't waste a moment. The wind seemed just as bad as before, but by staying close to the big stone structures they could avoid the worst of it. At least the rain had eased. Anywhere they found the big four-legs, they found food, and there were also the tracks that were used by the two-legs. Here they found the ground was worn down by foot traffic and by the wheels of their carts, so there were often stones to be dislodged, revealing all manner of creepy-crawlies. More than once during the morning they were startled by the two-legs suddenly coming round the bend, and had to take off in a mad hurry, all feathers and panicky cheows. During the afternoon the chows went further afield, flying over many stone structures that were grouped together and making the most dreadful racket. They could see some enticing looking grass in the distance and Yowynk went off ahead, keen to find out if it was worth a look.

The wind made flying twice as hard as usual, and he had to stay low or it would be even worse. With the big stone structures, and the smoke rising from them, the other three chows lost sight of him, staying in touch only by their cheows. And then it happened. Suddenly, mid air, something hit Yowynk. At the same time there was a noise, a bloodcurdling, deep, throaty sort of screech. It was a huge black bird, and it had got away with a beakful of his breast feathers. In a second, Yowynk lost control and tumbled, sprawling through the air. He righted himself, glanced up and there it was; a raven, coming right at him again, making a noise that could only be saying, "I aim to kill you." Everything was a mad blur for Yowynk. This was unlike anything he'd experienced before, and it was happening much too quickly to take in. The blood roared in his head, and for the first time he experienced the raw, sick sensation that was pure fear. His instincts took over, going into a neat dive to the left, then veering off to the right. But the vast, terrifying bird followed. It wasn't giving up that easily. Yowynk began to fear for his life.

At that moment there was a sudden, loud 'cheeoow!' In a split second Yowynk's three friends were alongside him, and then shooting upwards straight towards the raven. Yowynk saw Cara make contact, briefly stabbing into the raven's flesh with her sharp red beak, making it squeal with pain. The older chow managed to do the same, while Lowen wheeled and fluttered all around the raven so that it didn't know if it was coming or going. There aren't many more awe-inspiring sights than a handful of smaller birds defending their air space from a predator. The chows didn't really hope to do any serious damage to the great bird, but they were certainly showing it that a chow is a bird to be taken seriously. Chows have a great spirit, as great as any bird in the sky. As the raven disappeared into the distance it screamed with frustrated rage into the air, whilst the four chows landed in the nearest clearing. Any semblance of dignity had long gone for Yowynk, who landed awkwardly and didn't care who saw. Taking a deep breath, his confusion quickly turned to relief as he realised the raven was long gone, and that his friends had saved his life.

"Greatbill," cheowed the older chow.

"Thank you," replied Yowynk, quietly.

The chows called the ravens 'greatbills' because they really were the biggest and strongest of all the crows, with a huge and powerful beak. Yowynk remembered them from when he was younger. There had been another nest on a large ledge just outside the stinky cave, and it had belonged to a family of ravens. Although the youngsters had fledged quite some time before Yowynk, the raven family had remained in the area, and had never looked a threat. Yowynk had even liked them. But although the ravens themselves could soar quite beautifully, and appeared most of the time to be the most dignified of birds, he could now see that they had another side to them. The fact was that when a raven was hungry, they could use their size and strength to overpower smaller birds quite easily. They were stealthy. They could lull you into a warm feeling of security, then hit you in the air and rip you to shreds. The greatbills were no friend of the chow.

"Were you frightened?" Yowynk asked his sister Lowen later, when they'd settled for the night.

"I didn't really think," she cheowed. Yowynk's skin was smarting where his feathers had been ripped out. He stared ahead of him into the dusk, reliving the moment his life nearly ended. This was never going to happen to him again.

# Going Home

For several days and nights, the chows carried on roosting on the dilapidated old wall. The wind slowly died away until they were left in the cold, dark stillness of winter. They'd survived the great storm. The raven hadn't reappeared, and the two-legs didn't seem to be giving them any serious trouble, as long as they kept their distance. The big four-legs provided this modest chattering with enough to eat, so they were getting by. They even saw a number of other chows in the area, who, like them, had come inland to shelter from the storm. But the days were so short now that they had to feed as much as possible to get through the long, cold nights. And all the rain, combined with the feet of the big four-legs had made the ground horribly boggy in places, which is no use to a chow at all. Besides all this, it just wasn't home. The coast was where they belonged.

"Can we go back soon?" cheowed Lowen. "I do wonder what's become of our mother and father, and our brother."

"Let's head back tomorrow," the older chow replied. "This is no place for us. Strange things happen here."

And so, early the next morning, the four chows spent some time feeding on the patch nearest to their roosting spot, and then began the journey back to the coast. They wound their way back along the long, meandering valley that had given them such protection from the storm. They could fly much higher now that the storm had passed, which was just as well because there were plenty of two-legs about. From a height they could clearly see the tantalising sight of the sea, off in the distance.

Using their instincts to guide them, they took in familiar landmarks on the ground, whilst constantly noting the position of the sun, which nestled low in the sky amongst hazy streaks of cloud. The chows were all glad to be heading home. They flew with such an urgency that they felt they could go on forever, and rejoiced when they caught their first sniff of the fresh Atlantic breeze, which meant they were almost back where they belonged. When they reached the coastline they were going at such a pace that they nearly shot straight out to sea. But they managed to turn and land in time, right on the very edge of the cliff tops, where the land was covered in big four-legs, and there were countless other chows feeding and flying and enjoying this special place, which really was the best home in the world for a chow.

The four of them had made it to the green cliff tops without much regard to where they would end up. But now that they'd arrived, they saw that their sense of direction had been better than they'd realised. They were only three small coves along from the stinky cave.

"Let's go!" cheowed Yowynk, as they all took off together.

"Where to?" asked Cara, confused.

"Somewhere very special!" replied Lowen excitedly.

As they swooped over the last rocky outcrop, the pointy rock came into view. It was still covered in yellow lichen, just as it had been when the young chows had landed on it the day they flew for the very first time.

"There!" cheowed Lowen. Just then, they heard

in the distance the most almighty racket. All they could see was a mad flurry of a dozen or so gulls down on the ground. They appeared to be pecking at something, but it was such a crazy commotion that they couldn't tell what. The noise was actually the hysterical crying of a terrified chow. The four chows swooped down and could see a black-fingered wing occasionally breaking free from the squabbling gulls. Since they had no respect for the greedy gulls at all, and were sure the unfortunate chow would soon be dead if they didn't do something, all four descended at once. Yowynk was the first to make contact, digging his scarlet claws into the neck of a gull, making it scream an agonised, ghastly squawk. Yowynk liked the feeling, and didn't let go until the gull was well into the air, by which time all of its cowardly friends were also fleeing the scene. A couple of them tried swooping back in on the chows as soon as their backs were turned, but fled again when the older chow turned and launched herself straight at them with a blood-curdling "Cheeooow!"

The poor bird left on the ground was a sorry looking sight, slumped lifelessly with one of its wings spreadeagled across the ground. It was uttering little whimpering cheows. It looked as good as dead. And then as its four bold rescuers stepped gingerly towards it, it muttered, quietly, "Have they gone?" Yowynk and Lowen realised simultaneously who it was. It was Hogh.

"You! You lazy creature!" screeched Yowynk. "How could you let those greedy white ones sneak up on you like that? Where's your dignity? What would you have done if we hadn't come along?"

"I don't know. It's all so hard sometimes," was all Hogh could manage.

"Are you all right?" asked Lowen, a little more kindly.

"I think so. They hadn't been on me for long. I'd got a bit carried away you see. I found this huge pat of dung from the four-legs, and there were ants everywhere…"

"Can you fly?" interrupted Yowynk.

"I'll try," replied his brother. And so Yowynk, Lowen, Cara and Hogh flew directly to the pointy rock. Hogh looked a bit shaky as he had a few feathers missing, but looked otherwise all right. Pulling himself together a bit he asked, "Where have you been?"

"All over. We went inland to escape the storm. What did you do?"

"Nothing. Stayed here. I didn't leave the cave. Hardly ate a thing for days. It was awful," Hogh complained miserably.

Just then Lowen realised something. "Where's our old friend?" she exclaimed, "There's only four of us!" At this they all cheowed anxiously, and launched themselves into the air, flapping hard to gain height as quickly as possible. Within a second they had a good view along the rolling grassy cliff tops in both directions. And there was the older chow, way off in the distance, dipping and diving along the coastline, heading east, alone.

"Goodbye! Thank you!" the young ones cheowed, as loud as they could manage.

# Three Years Later

Three years had gone by. The young chows had all grown into handsome adults. Even Hogh. Their beaks were long and sharp, and a beautiful deep red, enabling them to prise out even the most reluctant ant. Their bright red legs were strong and powerful, and it felt like they could bounce around on them all day if they wanted to. Their plumage looked blacker than anything black you've ever seen, and it picked up beautiful blue-greens when they flew in the bright sunlight.

Cara had become Yowynk's constant companion, and they flew together all the time now. Sometimes they joined a large chattering of other chows, and sometimes they would recognise Yowynk's sister Lowen amongst them. She'd settled with her own mate further east. Whenever Yowynk and Cara found themselves amongst a large chattering, they'd find Hogh was with them. "Just follow this lot!" Hogh would cheow to his brother. "They'll find us plenty of food!"

Food was the one constant in Yowynk and Cara's

life. No matter what trials they'd been through, there was always enough food. Sometimes they'd had to search for it. Sometimes the grassy turf had been so hard or dry that they'd had to poke and prise twice as hard to get half as much. But they'd never really gone hungry. All animals need two things, above all else. Food, and shelter. The little insects that lived in the ground and among the rocky crevices of the cliff tops provided the food, and the stinky cave, below, provided the shelter at night. A pretty convenient arrangement, when you think about it.

As far as other dangers were concerned, Yowynk and Cara had managed to stay away from the black-cheeked peregrine. They'd learned that old Black-cheeks would always opt for easier pickings than a chow. What was the point in straining yourself chasing chows when a juicy dove was just as tasty, and twice as easy to catch? They'd certainly had plenty more scares from the greedy white gulls, with their foul tricks, and from the greatbilled raven, but nothing they couldn't handle.

Every spring, Yowynk's parents had returned to the stinky cave to patch up their old nest and raise a new brood. And now, three years since Yowynk himself had hatched in that cave, he and Cara built a nest of their own. They chose a ledge near the entrance, a good distance from his parents' nest, but sheltered enough from the Atlantic gales, and the unwanted attentions of those greedy white gulls. They did a pretty good job of it too, and were soon flying with four of their very own fledglings. They taught their young ones all about avoiding old Black-cheeks, and the greedy gulls, and the greatbills, and about how to preen and look after their feathers, and about where to find the leatherjackets, and when, and about a million other things. And when they met up with Lowen, she had young ones of her own too.

Over their many years together, some of Yowynk and Cara's youngsters did fall out of the nest, and one was even caught by old Black-cheeks, and one or two perished in flying accidents, and the greedy white ones occasionally got the better of a young chow and made a meal of him. But that's what happens, and nature is nature. Other creatures, after all, had to survive too. Yowynk and

Cara never went back to those alien places inland, because they never again experienced a storm as fierce as the one that came in that first winter. And so for the rest of their lives they rarely strayed far from the sea, even though chows needed little from it. And each year more and more chows filled the skies, because it was a good time to be alive.

BOOK II

# Popet

## 1900

# Two Naughty Boys

Two hundred years had passed since Yowynk's time. The stinky cave was still there, half way along the mighty cliff. The shingly stones would still wash in and out with the Atlantic breakers, and the sun would still fall at midday onto the pointy rock, which was still all covered with yellow lichen. It all looked just the same. And you're probably wondering if there was another nest on the craggy ledge in the stinky cave. Well, there was. Two hundred years after Yowynk had hatched, there sat another nest, just like Yowynk's nest. Except that this one didn't have any lovely soft sheep's wool lining it. Feathers and sprigs of heather were all that was making this nest soft for its occupants.

Inside the nest, sat two little chow chicks. There was a male chick, called Codha, and a female, called Popet. They had no brothers and sisters; it was just the two of them. They were to become good friends. The two little chows were getting ready to fly, just as Yowynk had done, and were doing a lot of wing-flapping and bobbing up and down. Their parents had been delivering food as quickly as they could, but were sometimes gone for quite a time. It was during one of these trips away that little Popet perched herself up on the side of the nest, and came as close as she'd yet got to jumping. She fluttered, and nothing happened. She shuffled about a bit on her still-brown feet, and thought about it again. Her brother Codha sat tight, just watching. Popet looked at the big white light, which was the entrance of the cave, and something in her knew that this was the place to go. Then, just as she was plucking up every bit of courage to make her first leap, she became aware of an unfamiliar sound below the nest. She looked down. And there, just below, was a young boy, looking up at her with his arm outstretched towards her, towards her home.

Popet screeched. Of course, she didn't know it was a boy. Only we know that. It was just a strange looking two-legged creature to her, a little chow chick getting ready to fly for the first time. And she didn't know that this boy and his friend had been waiting and waiting for the lowest of low tides in order to get into the cave, and even then they'd got quite wet clambering over some horribly slippery rocks. The boys were certainly determined. Popet didn't even know they meant her harm. As far as she knew, this was just the natural way of things. So she wasn't really too worried. She made another little 'cheeow' sound, and concentrated on getting launched again. And then she did it: she leapt upwards and dipped right over the boy's head. He swiped at her, but he was so taken by surprise that all he caught in his hand was air. Up and out Popet went, for the very first time, and onto the pointy rock, just as Yowynk had, all those years before.

The boy was standing on a wooden crate that he'd brought with him, and stretching up as far as he possibly could. His friend was standing below him on the shingly stones, watching. He was jumping up and down with excitement, egging the first boy on.

"Geddun! Geddun! There must be anuvver!" he shouted.

"I kent! 'tis too far up! I need a ladder!" replied the top boy, straining and stretching for all he was worth. With that, both parent birds flew into the cave, in that dramatic way that only a chow can, and saw the pair of big two-legs. They cheowed madly, circling in the air above the nest, not landing, because they knew only too well that the big two-legs usually meant bad things. They could see from above that only Codha remained in the nest and, of course, thought the worst. They'd completely missed Popet, sitting on the pointy rock outside as they'd swooped past. In less than a moment, the parents both landed on a little sill, a couple of metres above their nest.

"Come out! Flap your wings and come out!" they cheowed to Codha. Then they became aware of showers of shingle clattering off the cave walls and roof. The boys were throwing handfuls of it at the parents, trying to scare them out of the cave. It worked. Both birds recognised the dangerous situation, and flew straight out into the big white light. Codha watched them. Poor chows. They thought in those few moments that Popet had been killed, and Codha would be the next. Their first and only chicks. If their first brood of chicks didn't survive, they might never have more.

But when the parents swooped out of the cave and saw Popet sitting there, hopping about with excitement at her first flight, they were overjoyed, and cheowed like crazy. And a few seconds later Codha flew straight out too, and onto the flat top of the pointy rock. The family were reunited, and all was well. The top of the pointy rock wasn't only a good place to perch and preen in the sun, but it was well out of range of any naughty schoolboys.

The chows set about checking that their fledglings were all right, fussing over them and cheowing in a contented sort of a way. They were very proud parents. After a minute or two the naughty boys came running out of the stinky cave, feet crunching loudly in the pebbly shingle. The incoming tide was washing over their feet and they were quickly up to their knees in surf. The front boy was still flinging shingle in the vague direction of the chows. It clattered on some of the surrounding rocks, and landed with little plops in the great Atlantic, which barely noticed. The boy at the back was clutching his wooden crate. They were angry, those boys, not to have captured some chows. Not that the chows knew that. They didn't understand the strange behaviour of the big two-legs at all. All they knew was that a minute ago things had looked bad, and now all was well again in their world.

"Tide's comin' in too fast! Let's get seagulls' eggs!" yelled one of the boys. "I know where there's 'undreds!"

# Starving

The world that Popet and Codha were to grow up in was very different to the perfect one that Yowynk had known all those years before. For the first few days and weeks their parents would find what they could to feed the fledglings, but meals were few and far between. Some ants here, the odd earwig there. Oh, how those young chows would have loved a bulging beakful of fat, wriggling leatherjackets. But they just didn't come. The two young ones grabbed every morsel that their hardworking parents could find for them, but it was all such hard work. During those early days their father would have to go far away to find food, leaving his family quite vulnerable. But if he didn't go and leave them unprotected, then the chicks would fail to thrive. Their mother remembered the dreadful fear she had felt when they'd arrived back in the cave to find only Codha there, and she didn't ever want to feel that way again. She knew what to do. She always stayed near her chicks, and watched constantly for the greedy white ones, old

Black-cheeks, the sneaky greatbills and, of course, those strange big two-legs. She did a good job protecting her fledglings, and slowly, slowly, the young chows grew bigger and stronger, and soon it would be time to venture onto the grassy lands where the real food was; the lands that provided such a marvellous bounty for all the chows that had gone before them.

"It's time we travelled further now, little ones," cheowed their father, at last. "There's much hard work to be done."

But when the family began proper forays over the grasslands above the cliffs, they barely landed. Popet and Codha soon learned that there wasn't much food to be had in amongst the green stuff, so they flew on and on, further and further.

"The green stuff's no good here," their father would say. "It's much too long, you can't get to the ground. Let's stop here amongst these rocks; there may be some ants." How Popet longed to taste a nutritious, juicy leatherjacket or two, but she didn't argue. There were some patches of shorter grass here and there, where they'd stop for some time and get the chance to do what chows do best, which is dig for creepy-crawlies on the ground. But there were slim pickings. Very occasionally, they encountered another chow in these places, but any joy at coming across one of their own kind was overpowered by the race to grab the few bits of food. Arguments would break out when chows squabbled over titbits, which was most unbecoming. Who'd have thought that such a noble bird could behave in such a way. But there was only one reason, and that reason is always enough to make any of us squabble and fight... hunger.

The young chows paid attention to their parents. Hunger and hard work was all they'd ever known, so they didn't complain. They just assumed that this was the way things were. And slowly they learned their flying skills, and where they might find a modest meal, and they just about got by. Like all chows, their first love was flying, and the young ones learned to tumble and skewer and soar as well as any chow ever had.

Codha in particular evolved a flying style that seemed extreme even for a chow. He flew with an intensity that his parents had never seen before, as if every aerobatic movement mattered beyond anything else. His dives always started that bit higher, and ended that bit lower. It was an incredible thing to behold. He wasn't showing off, he just flew with a unique exuberance. He would stretch his healthy young wings a little further, so that they'd give him that extra bit of lift, which seemed to make all the difference. It made him fast, faster than any chow. At first Popet was a little jealous of her charismatic brother, but only a little. She and Codha were quite lonely in a land with few chows, so they grew very close, and Popet was proud that her brother was such an aerobat. When another chow occasionally flew past she'd see them looking over at Codha, who would usually put on an amazing display, and Popet would whisper to herself, "That's my brother."

But Codha would sometimes go too far. His dives were ending much too late, and sometimes he'd only just clear the ground at the last moment. More than once Popet had watched him become so carried away that he'd be tumbling within a wingspan of the side of a cliff. The way Codha flew was starting to scare Popet.

"Be careful, you're going to hit one of those rocks one of these days!" she'd warn him. "You shouldn't leave it so late! Be careful!" But he'd never listen.

Their parents often told them stories of the old days, the days when Yowynk was around. Stories that had been passed down from previous generations of chows, and no chow knew for certain if they were true. They were tales of a time when there were lovely short green lands as far as a chow could see, and you could stop and snack wherever you wanted. The skies had been black with chows, and they never went hungry. It sounded fantastic.

"Never mind," exclaimed Codha, "I'll find us a place like that! I'll look harder than any chow's ever looked!"

"Don't waste your time son," cheowed their mother. "Those times are gone, since the great four-legs left, and the green grew long. We just have to take what we can get now. We just have to look a bit harder." There were hardly any chows around anymore. Even three or four years ago their parents could remember seeing more of them in the skies, and roosting in all the crags and crannies, but now a chow was a rare sight indeed. Many had simply left in search of better territories. Plenty, especially the old and sick, had perished from lack of food during the bad winter months. And without sufficient food to sustain it any animal is more vulnerable, and less able to defend itself against attacks from predators. Just a few brave chows were still hanging on now, because, after all, this was their home.

# Leaving Home

After some weeks Popet and Codha started spending more time away from their parents, until they were able to completely look after themselves. Their mother knew this time had been coming. Parent birds become exhausted bringing up their young, what with all the nest-building, and the sitting, and the finding of food for the little ones, and the preening, and all the flying lessons. Birds are very hardworking creatures. So there always comes a time when they have to say goodbye, otherwise the parents would never survive. As this moment loomed, their mother had a quiet word with Popet.

"Please keep an eye on your brother. His flying frightens me. He's good, but he's so young. He won't know how hard something is until he hits it for the first time," she cheowed.

"I'll look after him!" Popet promised, flattered to be charged with such a grown up responsibility. And so the parents stayed in the area around the stinky cave, while Popet and Codha, the best of friends, left home to make a new life for themselves. They flew west on the first day, squinting into the setting sun and roosting on a ledge close to an outcrop of smooth boulders. The crevices that separated the big rocks provided the young chows with quite an acceptable supper of beetles and centipedes.

"Not bad for our first night away from home. I think we're going to be fine," cheowed Codha tenderly to his sister, aware that she was feeling just a little bit homesick.

The next day, their first day properly on their own, they continued west into areas they'd never ventured into with their parents. It was all very exciting. Although they only saw one other chow, it was a beautiful sunny day, and they were both loving being out on their own, all grown up. In the air they dipped and ducked, their fingers splayed, looking for the next feeding site, but really they were more interested in the sheer wonderful feeling of being in the air. Then Popet noticed Codha climbing to a great height.

"Oh no, here we go again," she muttered to herself. Sure enough, her brother tucked his wings back and dived. He plummeted so fast that even old Black-cheeks would have been given a run for his money. Then he stopped dead, and skewered, mid air, sideways, and rolled in the air a couple of times. Popet watched it all, amazed at his prowess, hating him for being so careless. "I'm supposed to be looking out for you, you stupid chow!" she muttered. At that moment there was a bang, the loudest bang they'd ever heard. Popet, stunned by the deafening noise, kept flying, with an eye on her brother. Something had happened to Codha. He'd lurched in the air, and a handful of feathers had shot from him. Yet he looked all right. Codha was wondering what on earth had just happened. "Never mind," he told himself, and continued the dive that he'd only been half way through. He wanted to prove that nothing could put him off his aerial duties, not even this funny clap of thunder that had happened in the middle of the day. But as he dived he realised something was wrong; he seemed to be veering off to one side, getting dangerously close to the side of some boulders. He couldn't tell why, but his body just wasn't behaving properly. He went to correct himself, adjusting his tucked-back wings, but he didn't do enough, spiralling into the ground, and coming to a sad, silent halt. Popet circled, way above.

"I told you! I told you! You never listen!" she cheowed. But Codha couldn't hear. She began her descent, but as she did so, she saw two big two-legs running towards her brother. From above she watched them gather him up off the ground, and put him into something, then walk away. As they did so, one of them looked up. In an instant, there was the terrible thunderous noise again. Popet didn't hang around. A chow knows when something isn't right, and she flew and flew as fast as her wings could carry her. As she flew, she cheowed great long, anguished cheows. But no other chow could hear them.

# Alone

"'ess, 'tis a chow all right," said the man. "Just a young 'un. See the beak, 'e ent proper red yet. 'e ent hurt neither, just stunned by the fall I reckon."

"Can I keep 'n, father? Can I? 'twood make a fiddy pet, an' 'twoont cost you nuthin'!" cried the boy.

"I dunno, son. These are gettin' some scarce these days. Reckon I could get a shillin' er so fer 'un. Fer stuffin' maybe." He peered into the leather satchel where Codha lay, blinking up at them.

"Oh please!" implored the boy. He was a quick thinker. "'e ent growed up yet any'ow. Nobody'd want a ol' chow with a lil' brown beak. Dun look nuthin' special! Let me keep 'im til 'e's proper growed up!"

"Well, we'll see," said his father.

\* \* \*

Poor Popet. She'd lost her best friend in the world. She couldn't accept that she was never going to see Codha again, so she landed as soon as she thought it safe, and tried to think things through. If it was you or me in this situation, we'd probably head straight back to our parents for some good advice and a friendly hug. But chows are proud and independent. Popet had left home, and that was that. She was going to make it through this. She knew how to feed herself, and her parents had taught her all about avoiding old Black-cheeks, and the greedy white ones, so she'd be all right. And sooner or later, she thought, Codha would show up again. He was a clever chow, for all his silliness.

So Popet found a nice ledge to roost on, next to a big clump of sea pinks. The ledge was sheltered from the north easterly breezes, and far away from the prying eyes of the big two-legs, whom she knew were bad. Her beak and legs were reddening nicely, and soon she'd be properly grown up. And so Popet got on with the business of being a chow. For the next few days she didn't stray very far from where the loud bang had happened, because she wanted to keep an eye out for Codha. She'd fly west along the cliffs for half an hour, then all the way back, and beyond, then back again. And the whole time she cheowed out the same message, the sound that meant "Codha! Codha!" But he never appeared.

Popet felt horribly alone. She didn't see a single chow for days. There were plenty of other birds, but she could never cheow to them. They had strange ways and languages she couldn't understand. She of course steered well clear of the greedy white ones. They revolted her, with their foul cackling and their filthy habits. They didn't seem to care how undignified they looked, or who saw them. And there were crows everywhere. But she belonged with chows, and there were none. She thought about Codha all the time. He was the only friend she'd ever had in her short life, and was starting to wonder if she'd see another chow, let alone her brother, ever again.

For a week or so Popet remained within an hour's flight of the big bang site. But she soon exhausted all the feeding places she could find. So one day, as she flew west on her usual forage, she carried on, and didn't return to the ledge next to the sea pinks. By the close of the day she'd ended up in a huge, gaping cove. As the shadows of the rocks grew longer and longer, she settled for the night on a west-facing cliff that caught the very last of the evening sun, bathing her in a soft orange light as it disappeared behind the horizon.

Next morning, the sun was well up and she was still slumbering. Because the cliffs faced west, it was very shady first thing in the morning, and she didn't notice how light it had become out over the Atlantic.

"Good thing my brother's not with me," she told herself cheerfully. "He'd have wanted to be out flying by now." But just thinking about Codha made her sad. There was no use pretending; she should just accept it. He was gone. Gone forever. Her spirits sank lower than ever. What was she going to do without him?

In her head she heard him crying out, cheowing over and over again. "Cheeoow! Cheeoow!" She could hardly bear that lovely, familiar sound rattling round inside her head, reminding her of her brother – and best friend – who was gone forever. Yet at the same time she rejoiced in it. The cheowing was becoming louder, and she realised with a start that she wasn't dreaming, and that it was the cry of a real chow! In an instant she took off, and spotted not one but two chows, not far away. They instantly heard her friendly greeting "cheow", and before long all three were making the sort of racket that a whole flock of jackdaws would be proud of. They swooped and tumbled, and probably flew a bit closer to each other than was healthy. They looked like a proper chattering. Neither of the birds was Codha, but at least they were chows! All three swooped onto a ledge together, and fussed and cheowed excitedly. The two birds were a young male, called Par, and his sister, Marthys. They were just a year older than Popet, with bright scarlet legs and beaks, and Popet couldn't take her eyes off them. She didn't even notice how awfully thin they both were. To her they were beautiful. And they seemed every bit as happy to see her as she was to see them. In a mad rush Popet excitedly blurted out her story, and where she was from, not caring whether her new friends could hear her properly. Par and Marthys had come from the west, where Popet and Codha had been heading. Things sounded bad out there too.

"The chows have all but gone from the west," explained Par. "The green is so long. Some perished over the short days, and some have gone in other ways."

"Any chows who have survived have moved inland," continued Marthys. "We're the only ones working our way along the cliffs, but it's getting harder every day." Popet didn't much care about how bad things had become for chows; she was too busy celebrating the fact that she'd found two friends. She quietly vowed to never let them out of her sight.

# The Cage

Little Codha, still a youngster, simply couldn't work out what had happened to him. He'd gone from being the fastest, cleverest chow in the sky, to this. First that bang, then the dizziness and everything went black, and now as he drifted back into consciousness, here he was, unable to move, in this sweltering, smelly old bag. He didn't even know what the bag was, or what these people were, but he knew that the bag had the stink of death about it. And his instincts were right. That bag had contained hundreds of dead animals in its time. Codha was terrified. He cheowed as best he could from inside the hideous bag, but he had no idea who to, or why.

The man threw his leather satchel down on the kitchen table, reached in and roughly grabbed Codha with both hands. Codha managed to wiggle a wing free, and flapped it wildly.

"We'll soon sort you out," said the man, reaching for a kitchen knife. " 'ere, you hold 'im down while I clip 'im. Stretch 'is wings right out mind."

"Careful father! You'll bust 'is wing!" cried the boy, mindful of his new pet. He watched as his father roughly lopped the ends off Codha's six beautiful fingers on his left wing. It didn't hurt him, but his heart was pounding like a drum, and he was mortified with fear. He let out a quiet, purring "cheow". It was all he could manage.

"'e ent goin' nowhere now," said the man. "If 'e tries, 'e'll just go in a circle!" With that he laughed a great loud belly laugh, which made Codha cheow again in quaking fear.

"'spose no-one'll want 'im stuffed with a knackered wing," the boy said, fanning the six chopped black feathers out in his hand. "'e don't look too purdy, with 'is knackered wing and 'is silly brown beak."

"'spose not," said the man, a furrow slowly forming on his heavy brow. He reached into his jacket pocket and took out a folded oily rag, in which was wrapped a small pocket knife, and a lump of black tobacco. Holding the tobacco in the palm of one hand, he began cutting it into tiny pieces with the knife. Then out of his top pocket he retrieved a dirty old clay pipe, which he packed tightly with the shredded black stuff. Scraping a match across the rough granite mantle above the fireplace he lit the pipe, drawing hard on it and quickly filling the tiny room with a thick fug of bluey grey smoke. He looked at his son, who was still gripping Codha tightly. "Heave 'im in the cage fer now," he declared, "I'm off to check me traps. Reckon we might 'ave a 'alf rabbit to go with that bit o' cabbage fer tea. Then I'm gonna make some enquiries down the tavern. Don't go feedin' 'im nuthin' from the larder mind. We ent goin' 'ungry fer no silly ol' chow. Find 'im some food from somewhere else." With that the man clamped his pipe between his teeth, picked up the awful leather satchel and left the room, slamming the door behind him.

The noise shocked Codha into making one more attempt at flapping his wings to free himself. It worked. Still pinned down to the table by the boy's small hands, he managed to free his stumpy clipped wing, which gave him the leverage to free the other one, and then with one mighty spring of his strong young legs, he launched himself from the table. But the boy was just as young and quick, and managed to grab Codha's tail just as he lifted off.

"Not so fast you ol' chow!" he shouted in surprise.

Still flapping like mad, Codha's clipped wing caught the boy's right ear. One of the clumsily-cut quills was sharp as a razor and sliced right through the boy's earlobe. He screamed with pain and shock, but he never let go of Codha. Despite the throbbing pain, and the tears pouring from his eyes, the boy carefully folded Codha's wings back, took hold of him firmly, and carried him over to the open door of a rusty old wire cage that sat on the room's only windowsill. He put him in and placed him gently onto the floor of the cage. He shut the door quickly for fear of Codha trying to escape. But he needn't have worried, because Codha just lay there on the floor of the cage, blinking, and letting out a very subdued, very sad little "cheeeoow".

The boy's whole head throbbed. He couldn't bear to touch his ear, it hurt so much. But he was aware of the damp sensation on his right shoulder, and could feel the blood trickling down his neck. He rushed to a wooden shelf on which there was a pile of folded rags, snatched at one, and grimaced as he pressed it to his ear. Then with his other hand he grabbed a rusty garden fork, which was so heavy he could barely lift it, and rushed out of the door.

# Going a Bit Far

Popet was overjoyed at meeting her new friends. For the whole of that first day they chatted and fussed over each other, finding what food they could in the area around the sunset cliff. When it was time to roost they were actually still quite hungry, because they'd not really been concentrating as much as they should have been. Par and Marthys liked it here, and certainly enjoyed young Popet's company, so they all agreed to stay together and really concentrate on finding a good food spot tomorrow. All three of them settled for the night together on the ledge on the sunset cliff. The jackdaws wheeled in the air and the sun became a tiny red spot behind a thin wispy line of cloud on the horizon. Two seals came ashore, a mother and her young pup, and settled for the night on the beach below. The chows didn't notice any of this, because they were too absorbed in each other's stories. Quietly they cheowed and cheowed, until they couldn't stay awake any longer. As twilight turned into blackness, and Popet fought to keep her eyes from closing, she thanked goodness that she was no longer alone. As sleep took her, she rejoiced in the sound of the great Atlantic rollers pounding away at the rocks below. A huge black-backed gull flew silently right over their heads, and out over the sea, briefly illuminated by the moonlight, until it slowly disappeared into the blackness.

For the next few days Popet, Par and Marthys explored the area. They would take a whole day to fly in a rough circle; west down the coast for most of the morning, picking at bits of food on the way, then they'd swing back in, sometimes quite a way inland, and back to the sunset cliff to roost every night. Along the way, each different type of terrain would reveal different birds. There were orange-billed oystercatchers down foraging on the beach. And when the chows found themselves crossing a bay to reach the next cliff, they could see shags and cormorants, guillemots and razorbills. Among the grass and the hedges the birds were smaller. Little ruddy-breasted, black-headed ones that made a noise just like when you bang two stones together, which we call stonechats, and the little linnet with its beautiful crimson breast that faded every autumn. Some birds they only glimpsed briefly, like the strange fellows we call whimbrel, and the little scampering dotterel.

The days went by quickly. Away from the sea they were discovering some quite decent places to feed. As usual, it was whenever they saw sheep and cattle that they knew they wouldn't go hungry. Unfortunately, when they came across these places, there were often people quite nearby. Popet was very wary of them. She'd told her new friends what had happened to her brother, and they were very sad for her. But they had a knowing look about them, as though they'd heard it all before.

One day they landed in one of their favourite fields, a good flat area contained within a dry stone hedge. It was very close to some big square stone structures, with plenty of people about. Jackdaws always seemed to be having a fine time amongst these places, but the chows sensibly steered clear. They were finding lots to eat in this particular field, where the grass was lovely and short, and there were plenty of sheep to keep it that way.

"The big four-legs are good friends to us, don't

you think?" cheowed Popet.

"Oh yes, go wherever you see them," replied Par.

"Out west we got so hungry that we would jump onto their backs! It's surprising what tasty little morsels you could find, if you were hungry enough," cheowed Marthys.

"Really? On their backs? What did the big four-legs do? Didn't they mind?" asked Popet.

"Not at all! They're our friends, remember?" cheowed Par, and they all cheowed excitedly. Popet had a thought. Maybe it was the spirit of her reckless lost brother, or maybe it was just her youth, but she felt she wanted to impress her new friends. Plucking up all her courage, she launched herself at the nearest sheep, landing rather gracefully on its shoulder. The sheep didn't seem to mind at all. Popet couldn't cheow anything, for fear of spooking the animal, but her friends soon spotted her.

"Careful!" cheowed Par straight away. "There are big two-legs very near!"

But Popet was busy trying to find the odd insect stuck in the sheep's fleece. It was quite a thrill.

Feeling confident now, she cheowed loudly, "You're right! The big four-legs really are our friends!" She hopped up and down the sheep's back, pecking wherever she thought she saw something move. What a feeling!

Suddenly there was an almighty commotion in the corner of the field, and all three chows were horrified to see a two-legs running towards them. In a split second, Popet's mind instinctively flashed back to what had happened to Codha. And this two-legs was much, much closer than the two that took Codha that day had been. Par and Marthys launched themselves into the air, heading directly away from the commotion, but as Popet went to take off, a claw snagged in the thick, thick fleece. She flapped and struggled desperately, but to no avail. The unfortunate sheep cried out, and Popet did the same, and an almighty cacophony ensued. The two-legs was almost upon her. And then at the last moment, in a mad panic, the sheep started to run away from the two-legs. The flapping chow and the advancing two-legs were just too much for it. The violent movements jerked Popet's claw free, catapulting her up into the air. She flapped frantically towards where her friends were circling high overhead on the other side of the field. On reaching them, all three flew away as fast as their wings could take them.

"Bleddy ol' craws!" yelled the man. "After they sheep's eyes! I'll get 'ee next time!"

The chows, of course, had no idea what they'd done wrong. But again, they'd had a first-hand lesson in steering clear of the big two-legs.

Sitting on their ledge later that evening, Popet was feeling quite embarrassed. Her friends were a year older than her, and she knew she'd acted foolishly. They had warned her, but she'd wanted to show off.

"I'm sorry," she cheowed, "I shouldn't have messed about so close to the big two-legs."

"Don't worry," replied Marthys. "At least they didn't go bang. That's when the bad things happen."

"I think we should be more careful than ever with the big two-legs in future. Nothing good ever happens around them," cheowed Par.

"Except that's where our friends always are, and it's them who keep the green short for us," cheowed Marthys. And they chatted into the darkness about the the big two-legs. Popet recounted the story about the boy trying to get to her the day she and Codha had fledged in the stinky cave. Par and Marthys were very interested, and had a similar story of their own.

"We had two friends out west," explained Par. "They'd roost in our cave with us. When the time came they built a nest, and a nice job they did of it too. Four eggs, and two proud parents. One day as we flew over we saw the big two-legs going into the cave, and we knew no good would come of it. Sure enough, we saw the father later, and he told us everyone had gone. The eggs, and his mate. He disappeared then, too. Well, what was there for him to stay for? No food out west, and now he had no mate and no eggs. We never saw him again." It sent shivers through Popet's feathers. She couldn't believe she'd been so silly, messing about with the big four-legs, so close to danger. Her friends had obviously been through some terrible things, and now she'd endangered them for no good reason.

"I'll never do anything like that again, I promise," she cheowed.

# A Reprieve

The boy's earlobe was healing well, but it was still awfully sore, and it was obvious that it would have that ugly split in it for evermore; even if he lived to be an old man. But there was no infection, and the boy had other things on his mind. He was much more interested in his new pet. A month had passed since Codha had been taken. He sat on the kitchen windowsill next to his cage, looking at the boy. The boy looked back at Codha, and held out a fine juicy worm. Codha gobbled it gratefully from his fingers.

"Hungry, Sparky?" said the boy. "I'll get 'ee some more when I'm diggin' fer 'taydies later." Codha gave out a little cheow, which the boy took to mean 'thank you', but actually didn't mean 'thank you' at all. Codha jumped over to the old kitchen table, where he started to gouge at the little gap between the rough planks.

"No more worms in there, boy," said the boy. "I'll 'ave to put you back in yer cage now. Father's 'ome dreckly. There'll be 'ell to pay if 'e sees you out. You should be stuffed in a glass case by now!"

The boy was a wretched looking specimen. The patches on the knees of his old grey flannel trousers looked as though they themselves needed patches. On his feet were black hobnailed boots that were at least two sizes too big for him. He'd stuff rags or paper in there to pad them out, so they didn't rattle about and give him blisters. Combined with his skinny frame, and his trousers that were too short, his huge boots gave him a comical look, like some sort of sad little urchin clown. He had jet-black hair, always carefully brushed in a neat, floppy side parting, which was almost as black as a chow's feathers, but nothing in the world is that black. The boy and his father lived in this one downstairs room alone, and slept in the one bedroom upstairs, which they reached via some rickety wooden steps. He didn't go to school, so any time he wasn't working for his father, he'd spend with his new friend.

Codha understood nothing of this bizarre new world, but he was slowly starting to sense that this two-legs was all right. He had no concept that the boy was his friend, and that he'd become the boy's pet, but an instinct made him understand that the boy was the sole source of his food, and was therefore extremely important to him. This strange two-legs spent hours every day talking to him, smoothing down his black feathers, and giving him titbits. Sometimes he would even pick the bird up and hold him whilst feeding him. Codha had flown onto his shoulder a couple of times, and soon learned that he'd be richly rewarded with insects whenever he did this.

Codha also learned that the boy was the only reason he was ever let out of the dreadful cage. He couldn't even stretch his wings in the cage, which, to a chow, is like torture. But every time the bigger two-legs went out of the door, the boy would open the cage and let Codha out. He would jump the short distance from the cage on the windowsill to the old plank table, then onto the granite mantle. From there he'd usually sit and look around the tiny room. Then he'd always jump back over to the windowsill, landing next to his cage. The first few times he'd done this he hit the window, thinking that this was his escape route. After a month he now realised that some strange force would always get in his way, and so he'd end up perched on the windowsill, because this was the closest he could now get to being outside. This little dark room was his home now, with all its strangeness; its sudden noises, and its smoke, and its floods of light whenever someone opened the door. Codha was very confused. He knew that this strange place was not where he was supposed to be, but he merely survived, constantly at the mercy of the big two-legs, living one day at a time.

There was a rattling at the latch and the boy's father thundered in, slamming the door behind him.

"I'm 'ome boy," he shouted, "'ave 'ee got they cabbages planted yet? We won't 'ave nuthin' to eat come springtime otherwise."

"I'm goin' out to start now," replied the boy.

"And dig up a good barrowful of 'taydies. See that you dry 'em out proper before you put 'em in bags mind!"

"'ess father. What 'appened 'bout the job? Did 'ee go lookin' up Wheal Polman?"

"There ent no job!" bellowed the man. "There ent no nuthin' up there! All the lodes is worked out. I tell 'ee boy, times is some 'ard. 'arder than I've ever known. Most o' the mines is shut down. We can't even afford to eat our own 'taydies. Thank God fer me traps. At least we can 'ave the odd rabbit. Pascoe'll be down fer 'is rent next week. I did 'ear a feller last night say a man from up England come down an' give 'im two bob fer a 'andful o' chow eggs. I couldn' believe it. Seems they'm so scarce they'm worth a fortune. I dunno where there's any left though. Last chow I saw outside was our one."

"I can keep ol' Sparky fer a bit though, can't I?" asked the boy, nervously.

"Nah, 'e's ready, I reckon. You've done some job feedin' 'im up. Looks like a proper 'ansum growed-up chow. Soon as I find the feller who wants 'im fer stuffin', I'll wring 'is neck, gentle like, so I don't mess 'im up."

The boy knew this was coming. Times *were* hard. A shilling or two for his pet chow was worth having. It seemed so odd to him that rich folks would pay good money to look at a dead chow in a case, though. If he was going to keep hold of his best friend he had to think quick.

"I could'n keep 'im fer me birfday, could I?"

"When is it boy?" replied his father, gruffly.

"Next Thursday. I'll be ten. I'd dearly love to keep 'im fer a pet. 'e ent no good fer stuffin' anyhow, 'cos we clipped 'im!"

" 'ess, all right," said the father, quietly. "Reckon 'e's a pretty good investment. They'll only get more scarce as time goes on, an' so I'll git more fer 'im. We'll wait 'til 'ee grows 'is new feathers dreckly, 'an then we'll see. You can 'ave 'im fer a present 'til the autumn. Don't go tellin' we've got a chow 'ere though. We don't want 'im took. Then if I can't sell 'im we can always eat 'im. I've 'ad worse." Plenty of people were having to eat anything they could trap or shoot, and this included crows. A chow probably wouldn't taste any different. The boy felt he would sooner starve than eat his pet, and was over the moon at this reprieve from his father. Codha was the best present he'd ever had.

"Thank you father!" he shouted, and ran outside to start digging potatoes. In his pocket was a little round rusty tobacco tin with a screw top lid. He called it Sparky's tin, and by the end of the afternoon it would be bursting with worms, beetles and grubs.

# The Gin Trap

Chows understand how long a month is, because of the new moon, which happens every month. And obviously they know a lot about how long a day is. But a chow is much more interested in years, because that's how they measure their lives. To a chow, there are countless little instincts that make them do things throughout the year, like natural triggers, each going off at the right time. And so a chow will know the time to start building a nest, the time to lay eggs, the time to start moulting so it can grow fresh new feathers. At any given time of year, it knows what grubs should be available, and where to get hold of them, and how deep to dig, and where to go if it can't find them. And a chow knows many other things too, tiny things that we can only guess at, because we are not a chow. They don't call it a year, like we do, but they know when one has passed. In the spring, the days get longer and warmer, the nights shorter, and most plants put on all their growth before getting ready to make flowers. And the chows don't miss a thing.

Popet, Par and Marthys had been together a year. They'd seen the whole cycle of things, and the way that this place was, all year round. They'd all agreed that this was the best place any of them had found. They roosted every night on the sunset cliff, and foraged by day wherever they found the big four-legs. It was always hard work finding food, but they were surviving. They even tried tasting other foods. Not the foul things they'd seen the greedy white ones picking at, but berries, and the crunchy dry seed heads of grasses. Some birds seemed to love them, although to a chow they tasted disgusting. But at times they had been grateful for anything to fill their bellies.

There were many hazards. There was always a threat from the black-cheeked peregrine, the gulls and the ravens, so they could never relax. And then the winter rain and gales would force them to take shelter when they knew they should be out finding food. But it was always the big two-legs that they feared most of all, because they didn't understand him.

One particular day, they were working their way across a nice short-cropped field. It was starting to spit with rain, and the clouds on the horizon were growing darker and darker. Rain was a mixed blessing for a chow. The wet would moisten the ground and make it much easier to stick their long beak into, so the insects would be easier to find. But at the same time a chow wasn't a goose; they didn't have webbed feet for paddling about on boggy ground, so they didn't enjoy such conditions at all. The three friends came to this particular field quite a lot, and they knew that the big four-legs had been there for a good few days, although they'd moved on elsewhere now. Again they knew that the two-legs were never far away. They'd even spotted one in that very field the previous evening, fiddling with something by the hedge. But the food was too good to miss, and they knew they'd have to take shelter soon, so they worked their way across the field, prising and gouging, and taking whatever they could find. All the time they cheowed and chatted.

"Over here! Look at this fresh earth!" cheowed Marthys excitedly.

"No! Too near the edge!" Par replied, ever watchful for danger. "That's where we saw the big two-legs!"

"Come away!" called Popet, even more frightened. But Marthys was tucking into a rich seam of ants, and she was getting quite carried away. Popet thought she'd lead by example. She jumped up, caught a waft of air, and was airborne, squinting into the driving rain.

"Come on you two! There's plenty more over here!" she cheowed loudly. Par saw what Popet was doing. He reckoned his sister wouldn't want to be left behind, so he followed Popet into the air and across the field. Just then, there was a sickening crack behind them. Not like the bang the big two-legs made; it was more like a stick breaking underfoot, but fifty times louder. Popet and Par knew immediately that something awful had happened. Even though the big two-legs weren't around, they both knew that this would be their work.

"Stay over here!" cheowed Par to Popet. "I'm going to see!"

Popet remained circling over the other side of the field, not daring to look, as Par flew back, fighting the gusting rain. He saw Marthys lying motionless on the ground where she'd been foraging, right by the hedge. Some sort of ugly black contraption appeared to be attached to her. Par didn't land, but let out the most terrible "Cheeeeeoow!!" in mid air. In a second he was back with Popet, flying past her, at great speed. "Come on! We've got to go! Come on!" he screamed to her as they sped back towards the sunset cliff.

Later, sitting on the ledge of the sunset cliff, Popet tried to get Par to tell her what he'd seen. But Par wouldn't explain anything, except for quietly murmuring, "She's gone. My sister's gone." Popet, of course, had a good idea how he felt. She'd long since given up hope of ever seeing her brother Codha again. They'd each lost their best friend, and to the same enemy, the dreadful two-legs. The salt rain was driving in from the sea now, and they cowered together on the ledge. Popet couldn't think of anything to say. She didn't really know what it was that had killed Marthys, and didn't want to know. Whenever the big two-legs was involved, horrific things would happen; things that never made sense. So she just snuggled up next to Par, and drifted into a fitful sleep. Par stared out to sea.

What could they do? It seemed like there was nowhere they could go where they would be safe. A chow had to eat, had to survive. But it was just becoming so hard. All enjoyment in the world, in being a chow in this beautiful place, was gone for Popet and Par. Even the warmest days, when they found food, and roosted with full bellies, became hollow and meaningless. Once in a while they would see another chow in the distance, flying on to somewhere new, but they would never stop.

To make matters worse, other animals didn't seem to be having any such problems. In particular, there were crows everywhere. All sorts of crows. They were as plentiful as the bits of foamy spume that the stormy sea would whip up into the air in a million tiny pieces. It seemed that just as chows were all gone, the other black crow birds were having the time of their life. Sometimes Popet and Par felt swamped by a world full of jackdaws. These stumpy-beaked silvery crows, with their piercing, pearly white eyes were never far away. Great flocks of them were constantly wheeling around them, making a colossal racket. They were impressive fliers too, and sometimes Popet felt tempted to fly with them. But that was a ridiculous idea. They may have been a type of crow, just as she and Par were, but they were worlds apart. These pesky jackdaws were always in the way, flying like manic little mini-chows, jerking this way then that, always cackling in their mad, high-pitched language. Oh jackdaws were good fliers all right, but they wouldn't ever flow effortlessly through the air like a chow. Popet realised how absurd it was to enjoy the company of jackdaws.

And there were carrion crows. Never in big flocks, but often working in pairs; the chows had many a run-in with one of these dark, devious fellows as they tried to rob them of a precious creepy-crawly. Then there were the rooks to deal with. Now here was a bird who always seemed to be having a good time. The way their great oversized beaks merged into their bare, featherless faces made it look as if they'd just strapped the silly things on for the day. And of course there were the great big ravens. Popet and Par knew all about them. There was often a cheeky magpie about the place too, strutting about in its black-and-white gangster plumage, always on the lookout for an opportunity to steal something from under another bird's beak. Crows, and yet more crows. They were so many types of crow.

How Popet and Par yearned for their own kind. As far as they were concerned, it was starting to feel as if they were the only chows left in the world. They carried on going through the motions of living, but without any passion. It was all very well for the gulls and the jackdaws, but the poor chows, who had to work so hard for their food, found that with each passing day, everything became harder.

# A Good Investment

It was the afternoon of the boy's eleventh birthday. He was walking home from the tin mine where he now worked every day. His job wasn't much, after all he was only a boy, but it brought in a few pennies a week, and it was better than nothing. He worked in the deafening stamps of the mine, where the great pieces of rough ore were brought from the ground and pounded into powder by the big iron crushers. The boy would clean, push barrows, fetch and carry, and do whatever he was told. For a skinny little boy he certainly got a lot of work done. It was a three-mile walk home, and he'd been up since five, so as he approached his father's tiny cottage he stopped and sat on the edge of the granite water trough at the end of the lane and stretched his legs. A little robin came straight to him and sat on his bony knee.

" 'ello little one. Now let's see, what 'ave we got 'ere," whispered the boy to the robin, slowly taking his baccy tin from the top pocket of his brown corduroy jacket. He unscrewed the lid and gave his red-breasted friend a good-sized worm. "You can't 'ave no more, mind. There's someone needs these more than you. Now go on and find yer own." The robin swallowed it all in two gulps, gave a little chirp and went on his way. The boy got to his feet and carried on up the lane, clumping in his great boots, which were still too big for him.

Rattling the front latch, he opened the door just wide enough for him to slip inside, and quickly closed it again. Within an instant, Codha landed on his shoulder.

"'ello Sparky!" said the boy.

"Cheeow!" replied Codha, as he plunged his long red beak straight into the boy's top pocket.

"Not so fast!" laughed the boy, as Codha dug his claws into the worn left shoulder of his jacket. He yanked the tin out with his beak, and then, using his beautiful broad wings for balance, daintily hopped with it onto the old kitchen table. The boy watched him as he tried to prise the lid off, and then in frustration started banging it on the tabletop, hopping from side to side constantly.

"I'd better take that, or they creepy-crawlies'll be all knocked out, not wrigglin' like you like 'em!"

The boy gently took the baccy tin, unscrewed the lid and sat down with it.

"Cheow," called Codha, impatiently. Sitting on a little wooden stool, with Codha on the kitchen table, the boy fed him the contents of the tin, bit by bit, until they were all gone. With every morsel the boy would quietly say "There".

Codha was used to this system. For over a year, he'd been almost entirely fed on little insects, and had become a handsome looking bird as a result. He'd get some mashed up hard boiled egg every few days, when the chickens in the back yard laid an extra one that his father wouldn't miss. Occasionally he'd get a bit of cheese or fat, but food was so scarce that he seldom got a look in. Besides, the boy spent such a lot of time working in the garden that it was never any trouble to pick up a suitable little insect every time he saw one. In no time he'd have a tinful, more than enough to keep a pet chow fit and healthy.

"I'm gonna 'ave to start puttin' you back in yer cage soon, Sparky," said the boy, "Father'll be 'ome dreckly an' 'e must'n see you out. 'e said 'e'd be gone a week, and it's been that."

The boy prayed every day that his father would come home with money in his pocket, but he never seemed to find work when he went looking. In the old days it wasn't a problem. There was work to be had in the mines, never well paid, but always there. And there was the odd less conventional way of making a shilling. The father knew plenty of men and boys who used to go and get clutches of chows' eggs for people. Collectors would pay good money in the old days for specimens to complete their collections. It was dangerous work, often abseiling down from the top of a cliff with a frayed old bit of rope to where the clever chows had built their nest, out of harm's way. The father knew a man in the village who'd broken his back doing it. But generally it had been worth it for a shilling or two, in those tough, tough times. And then there was always the occasional shipwreck. The father had seen all sorts washed up after a winter wreck, and it was generally accepted that the locals would take what they could find. Occasionally it might be something you could sell, but usually it was either consumed or used by the people who found it. Alcohol, meat, timber, fruit, they'd all helped relieve their poverty. But now there weren't even as many wrecks as there used to be. It was becoming harder and harder to get by.

The boy had been through a lot in his eleven short years. He hadn't even known his mother, since she'd died in childbirth. His father had crushed his hand at work shortly afterwards, and it had been no good for grabbing much ever since. Although he talked constantly about finding another proper job, the boy suspected that his father was unemployable for any decent mining work. He'd never be able to get up and down the ladders, let alone do anything else. But his father was a proud man. He wouldn't do any old job. Fetching and carrying wasn't for him. They'd lived in a cottage in the village when the boy was very little. They'd had friends, and been part of a community. But then they'd been thrown out by the landlord because it was just the two of them, and a family of eight or ten could fit in the space. And so they'd ended up in this tiny cottage, which was really little more than a hovel. They had no neighbours. So who could blame the boy for growing so close to his special pet? He really didn't like to imagine life without him.

Codha, meanwhile, knew nothing of this. All he knew was that his big two-legs friend who fed him seemed to be acting very oddly indeed, letting him out to fly around the room for days on end, and then locking him up like this. What a strange, strange world this was. At night Codha would dream weird, half-remembered memories of his parents, and his life with his dear sister Popet. He even had hazy visions of the stinky cave. And he could still smell it. Most powerful of all were his memories of flying; and the sensation of really soaring in those salty air currents, out there above the cliff tops, where he belonged. He'd never forget that. Not until the day he died.

In the year or so that Codha had been locked in this small, dark, smoky cottage, he'd started to sense that it was going to be the only life he'd ever know. He had no idea that he was living on borrowed time. The father knew that he'd made a mistake in letting his son grow to love his pet chow, but was now using the situation to his advantage. Codha was a beautiful looking bird now, with the blackest, glossiest plumage you've ever seen. He was blacker than the blackest black, if you can imagine that. It was all because of the love Codha was getting from his son. During the summer months, Codha had gone through the moult. He'd shed each of his old, tired feathers one by one, and grown a shiny new one in its place. There were so many old discarded feathers flying about the place that it was all the boy could do to collect them up off the floor every day so that his father didn't suspect that Codha had been let out of his cage. Although Codha had grown splendid new wing feathers, they didn't need to clip him again, because as far as the man was concerned, he never left his little cage. The boy's father believed that with his handsome new wings Codha was becoming a seriously valuable bird.

"Never let 'im out the cage, mind," he'd told his son before he went. "I'm gonna find out where I can get rid of 'im while I'm away, either alive or dead."

Now that a week had gone by the boy reluctantly squeezed Codha back into his awful cage, and awaited the return of his father.

Sure enough, at the end of the following day, his father returned. "How've you been, boy?" he said.

"Very well, thank you father," replied his son, ignoring the smell of beer on his breath. "Any jobs goin' out there?"

"Damn 'ee boy. I told you before, there ent nuthin' out there. So I 'ope you bin workin' 'ard. You bin up the mine every day like a good boy?"

"Yes sir, just like you said."

"There's good news about ol' Sparky though, boy." The boy's blood ran cold. These were the words he'd been dreading. "I met a chap up Luggan who reckons 'e got two bob fer an ol' chow 'e caught in his rabbit trap. An' it was all busted up, where the jaws 'ad snapped on 'un. 'e reckoned we could name our price if we found a live one, a fit one like. Reckoned there's none left no more. We're sitting on a little gold mine 'ere boy. Wheal Sparky, that's what we'll 'ave to call 'im!" The man guffawed at his own wit. The boy was running out of ideas. He knew that his father was tempted to keep Codha for longer to make more money. But he also realised that sooner or later when things got really bad, and he needed the money, his father would suddenly lose patience. It could happen any time.

# No Hope

A year had now passed since the death of Par's sister Marthys. Every day Popet and Par would work the fields. They'd watch the sky for old Black-cheeks, and the horizon for the greedy white ones, and for any sign of the big two-legs. But every minute of every day, they were scared. They simply didn't know when it might happen again. It could be a big bang, like the one that took Codha, or a big crack, like the one that took Marthys. They often heard the big bangs. A couple of times they'd heard one and then seen a crow go still and fall out of the sky, just as Codha had done. They couldn't work it out at all. There would be no warning, no clue. They didn't eat as much as they should have, because they were looking all around them for danger, when they should have had their beaks buried in the soil in search of juicy leatherjackets. So they looked thin. Neither of them realised it, because they'd both forgotten what a chow was supposed to look like. There was no sense to the world at all for poor Popet and Par.

They still roosted on the ledge on the side of the sunset cliff, where they would quietly cheow to each other, aware that they'd both been through the same awful experience, but not really discussing it. Popet and Par grew very close, each knowing that they had no other friend left in the world. When the time came, some deep instinct rose in them both and they felt a powerful force to start nest-building. Neither chow could explain it, nor understand it. They didn't even discuss it, but every moment they weren't feeding themselves they'd pick up a stick, or yank at a root, for they knew, deep down, that this is how a chow's nest must be constructed. They even started to return to the ledge on the sunset cliff with these bits, and they carefully began positioning them there, pecking and tugging and forming the skeleton structure of a nest.

But the chows were thin, and weak, and it was taking all their time just to find food. All this extra exertion going into nest-building didn't make sense. There was too much danger about, and not enough food to be thinking about all this extra work. And so an instinct even stronger than the one to build a nest rose within them. It was the pure survival instinct. After a few days they didn't pick up any more sticks, or tug on any more roots. They just carried on feeding, and flying, and feeding some more. The sad beginnings of their nest sat forlorn on the ledge on the sunset cliff, and slowly fell away. Some bits were even taken by the greedy gulls for their own nests. They'd steal anything, those wicked birds.

One evening the two chows were sitting on the ledge on the sunset cliff waiting for sleep. All the sticks were gone now, and everything was back to normal. Popet moved closer to Par, so they could benefit from each other's warmth. Not a day ever went by when Popet didn't think about her lost brother, Codha. Often when she shut her eyes she would see him, tumbling absurdly through the air, then stretching those beautiful wings and rocketing upwards, the way only Codha had ever done. But she no longer thought of him in terms of being alive. Too much time had passed.

Suddenly Par cheowed, quietly, "Do you still think about him? Do you still dream you'll see him again some day?"

"I'll never see him again. We'll never see any chow again. It's just us," replied Popet, sadly. With this a flock of fifty or so cackling jackdaws flew past, very close.

"Do you think we're the only chows left in the world?" Popet wasn't used to this sort of talk from Par. He was usually so steady, so reliable. She didn't like it. It made him look vulnerable. And if Par was vulnerable, she felt vulnerable too.

"I don't know," Popet replied. "What does it matter?"

After some time Par cheowed, "You know I'll look after you don't you? I'll always be there. Always."

# Out of Time

"Over two years we've 'ad this damn bird, boy. It's time fer 'im to go." The boy's father looked sure this time.

"Why? Why can't he stay? I get food fer 'im every day, it don't cost you nuthin' still."

"I know that, boy. You've done a good job, I'll say that fer 'ee. But 'e's stinkin' up the place, an' you can spend yer time doin' proper work, not diggin' worms all day. Times is 'ard, remember."

"I know the real reason!" blurted the boy, unable to contain his anger. " 'tis money! That's all 'tis! 'e's my best friend, an' I had 'im fer me birfday! Two birfdays! 'e dun cost us nuthin'! Please!" The tears were coming now, because the boy realised that the situation was hopeless. He'd heard in the village that a well spoken gent from up country had been in the tavern saying that he wanted a chow for his collection. A stuffed one. The boy knew the amount his father had been offered for Codha. It was an offer he couldn't refuse.

" 'tis all too late son. I done the deal. Kent back

out. Sat'day night I'm deliverin' 'im, alive, down the Tinners Arms."

"No! You kent! You kent!" was all the poor boy could sob. It was Tuesday. Four days was all the time he had left with his best friend. Meanwhile Codha blinked out from his tiny cage. His borrowed time had run out. His destiny was confirmed.

Next day the boy's father was out for the day, so as soon he got back from the mine, the boy let Codha out of his cage. The chow had become like a brother to him, and he simply couldn't work out what to do about this awful situation. He'd lain awake all night staring into the darkness while his father snored, praying that there might be a solution out there somewhere. Yet it wouldn't come to him. The boy had never harmed Codha in any way, other than when he put him in the cage, which was for his own good. And the boy was proud of his pet. Hardly anyone had ever seen Codha, because no-one ever came to the cottage, but still the boy was proud of him. He couldn't have looked after him any better. If only the boy had known that Codha had once been the most fantastic flier, even amongst other chows, well, he would have been even prouder. Codha hopped straight onto his shoulder and stayed there while the boy paced around the tiny room, first one way, then the other.

"What we gonna do, Sparky, eh?" he said desperately.

"Cheow," cheowed Codha, which meant "Where are my creepy-crawlies, I'm starving!"

On Friday evening the father was leaving for the night, as he usually did.

"I'm takin' 'im tomorrow night mind, boy," he said. "Bedder say yer goodbyes by then. I'll be back tomorrow af'noon." He left the cottage, slamming the door behind him. The boy went straight to Codha's cage and let him out. But this time Codha didn't jump onto the boy's shoulder, or onto the old pine table. He didn't even fly to the drain by the back door, where sometimes the boy left his baccy tin of creepy-crawlies. Today, Codha simply hopped onto the windowsill, next to his cage. He perched there, his back to the room, just staring out at the view. He'd long since given up any idea of flying out there, as he knew he'd meet that strange invisible force blocking his way. The boy wondered what was going on. "What you doin', Sparky? I got creepy-crawlies 'ere!" But Codha didn't seem interested in food, or the boy, or anything in the room. He seemed only interested in the outside, the place where he hadn't been for over two years. Two years. In that time he hadn't sniffed the air, or felt a breeze ruffle his feathers, or even seen another bird, let alone a chow. The boy climbed the rickety wooden steps to bed, leaving the baccy tin on the table, half full of insects. He left the lid screwed on just enough to prevent the insects from crawling out, but loose enough for Codha to remove it when he grew hungry.

Next morning Codha was still standing there on the windowsill, looking out. The tin on the table was untouched. The boy sat down on the stool, his elbows on the table and his chin resting on his cupped hands. He'd never seen anything like this. For twenty minutes he sat there, just watching Codha on the windowsill. And slowly he started to realise. The boy's face changed. For days he'd had a troubled expression that made him look much older. But now he looked like a boy again. His face cleared, for now he knew what to do. Just like that. He stood up, and calmly walked to the window. Carefully leaning across Codha he brushed the cobwebs away, undid the rough iron bolt and opened the window. Codha was immediately hit by an exhilarating rush of cool sea air. The sensation brought a great flood of memories straight back to him. The boy could hardly breathe. All his emotions were churned up inside him. He knew that he would be thrashed within an inch of his life for this. But a thrashing would mean nothing compared with losing his best friend in the world. But losing his best friend in the world and knowing he was still alive, well, that was much better than losing him and thinking of him stuffed, in a glass case.

Codha turned around to face the boy, gave a loud "cheeooow", and hopped over to the tin of creepy-crawlies. He quickly flipped the lid off and worked his way through the whole lot, that hungry chow. Then he flew onto the boy's right shoulder, claws digging into the corduroy material that he'd worn away over two years. He gently nibbled the boy's sorry-looking earlobe with his beautiful scarlet beak, gave another little cheow, then hopped back onto the windowsill, and out of the window. The boy watched as his friend swooped over the front vegetable plot, and out in the direction of the sea, disappearing around a big patch of furzey bushes. Tears were running down both the boy's cheeks. But they were not tears of sorrow.

"Bye Sparky," he whispered.

# Winter

The days were getting shorter now, and the fresh winds off the Atlantic started to cut through Popet and Par's plumage, even when they fluffed themselves up to protect against it.

"The long nights are on their way," cheowed Par. "There'll be less time to feed. We should be eating as much as we can now."

They were exploring some new terrain back east along the coast. It was a bit too far from the sunset cliff, really, but was the only stretch of land they could find with short cropped grass on it. There were few leatherjackets to be found in the short grass this time of year, but they found some fairly good-sized centipedes and some decent beetles. This new place also had several areas where big granite boulders were piled high on top of each other, enabling a chow to forage in amongst their crevices. Everywhere along the coast the big four-legs were gone, apart from this one spot. The chows had no idea why they'd all gone, but there was nothing they could do about it.

"Better head home," cheowed Popet, "the sun's getting low." The two sad chows heard the now familiar bangs in the distance as they flew back east to the ledge on the sunset cliff that looked like it was to be their home forever.

"Perhaps we should think about heading back further east," cheowed Par as they settled on the ledge. "After all, it's where I was heading when I met you. You could show me the cave. The one you were hatched in."

"Perhaps," replied Popet. "Anything's got to be better than this. Let's see when the days start to get longer." Poor Popet was almost past caring. They communicated with each other less and less these days. Other than the essential cheowing that was necessary when in flight, which constantly informed each other of where they were, they didn't bother much with conversation. In reality they were both tired of life. Memories of their youth, when they remembered seeing other chows, had all but faded away. It seemed they now existed in a world without food, and where danger lurked around every corner. While other birds thrived, the two poor sad chows scraped by in this alien world, like ghosts from another time.

Every day for a week or so, the chows worked over this new terrain. One chilly autumn morning, they were busy at work among the crevices of the big rocks, dislodging small stones as they went and pecking madly at the ground as the tasty cocktail of creepy-crawlies all scurried for cover. Just then Par noticed a twitching in a nearby hedgerow. Whenever they noticed any movement that they weren't sure about, they'd take off and not return for some time. Although so far they'd managed to elude him, they were both terrified of the big two-legs, and never knew when he might strike again. So without thinking, Par shot into the air, cheowing to Popet as he did so. Popet followed suit, and within seconds they were high in the sky, safe from any danger on the ground. They both looked down to see what the fuss had been. Suddenly Popet called out "There! Just a big four-legs, stuck in the sticks!" They both breathed a sigh, relieved that they hadn't just been so close to danger. It takes a chow a little while to get over an experience like that, and they remained in the air for some time, while they decided where to go next. Then they both heard a noise. It was a noise that they both knew, but for a second they couldn't place it. It was extremely familiar, yet at the same time it was something they hadn't heard for a long, long time. Then, both at once, Popet and Par realised what it was, and started cheowing uncontrollably. It was the sound of a distant chow.

They looked, and saw it, the unmistakable swooping flight of a chow. Then Popet went quiet. Par glanced at her, and then back at the lone chow. At first he couldn't believe it was any kind of bird he'd seen before, but the bird was cheowing the whole time. It was flying like nothing Par had ever seen. Great exaggerated swoops, one after another, then in one deft movement it would tuck its wings back and fly almost vertically upwards. Par couldn't believe what he was seeing. Nothing could fly like this. At least, nothing he'd ever seen. It wasn't possible. And then time would seem to stand still as the chow appeared to hang motionless in mid air, and then plummet. Par glanced again over to Popet and saw that she was transfixed, staring at the bird. "It's… It's……" was all she could manage to cry. The lone chow kept its distance, but then, quite suddenly and without warning, it ceased its playful dipping and swooping, and headed purposefully straight towards Popet and Par at incredible speed. Par could see that it was a beautiful bird. It had been a long time since he'd seen a healthy chow, but he couldn't remember them looking like this. And now Popet was off, swooping towards the lone bird in her own way. And Par understood. He watched as Popet reached him and they tumbled together, falling as if they would fall forever, cheowing and chuckling as they dropped, then in perfect unison they both righted themselves and swept upwards joyously. They looked as if they'd been practising together all their lives. Par watched it all, and when he felt the moment was right, approached.

Drawing alongside the new arrival he called out, "It's very good to see you. Welcome back."

BOOK III

# Dirak
# & Bir

## 2001

# Shadows in the Sky

For all those years, the poor chows had been shot for sport, and trapped, and kept as pets, and poisoned, and even eaten. Then, as they started dying out, and there were only a handful left, people had even wanted to stuff them to show off in a glass case. Or they'd try to get to their nest to steal their eggs. Imagine! Truly, it seems like just about anything bad you can think of had been done to the poor chows. Popet, Par and Codha had been among the very last chows left in Yowynk's land. And now they'd died out. Completely. There wasn't a single one left.

But just as the last few disappeared, the strangest thing started happening. The people who lived in Yowynk's land began to realise that chows are a most special bird. They even started to say things like, "Well, the chows really belong here you know", and "If only they hadn't all been killed and driven away". You'd see pictures of chows on books, and on coats of arms, and on pub signs. People were now using the chow as a symbol for the very land itself. Some believed that when King Arthur was killed in ancient times his soul had become a chow. The chow was revered now, and people lamented the fact that it was gone forever. Things certainly were different without them. The place seemed sad. There had been no bird like it. Boring old crows and rooks and jackdaws were all right, but the sky came alive when a chow flew across it. You'd know if you'd seen one. You have? Well then you do know. People wanted things to be the way they'd been in Yowynk's time. They wanted to see the skies alive with chows again, so everyone could see them tumbling through the air, cheowing like crazy and living a happy life. They prayed the chows might come back some day, and wondered if there was anything they could do to encourage them. They watched the cliffs, hopefully.

But all they could see were shadows in the sky.

# Four Good Friends

Although they were all gone from Yowynk's land, chows still existed in other places. Far away in the distant mountain ranges, you could find plenty of them. This was the land of Yowynk's ancient ancestors, where all chows had once lived, thousands of years before. Closer to home, there were a few small groups here and there in other lands, living along the cliff tops where the terrain was the way they liked it, with short, grazed grass and rocks to forage amongst.

A hundred or so miles south across the sea from Yowynk's land, on the southwest coast of a place we know as a different country altogether, there was a little community of just a few dozen chows. Life was hard for this group, almost as hard as it had been for poor Popet and Codha. They too were finding it increasingly difficult to get by, and every day they struggled. People weren't out to get them as they had been in those bad old days, but they were causing problems for these chows in other ways. The area where the chows lived was very pretty, and more and more people were wanting to spend time in pretty places. They wanted to swim, and sunbathe, and go boating, and fishing, and kite-flying, and, well, who could blame them? But unfortunately the chows didn't want to join them. Chows, after all, are animals, and they just wanted to do what they'd always done. They wanted to peck and forage in the short, short grass, and tumble with each other through the fresh, salty air, and roost in among the cliffs. That's all. But they were finding that wherever they wanted to go, there were people.

This would happen at the most unfortunate times. Just when a pair of chows was busy nesting and trying to raise their young ones, that's when all the people would start arriving, because the days were warmer, and it was their holiday time. A chow would be busily gouging at a promising-looking anthill, trying to find enough to feed his hungry chicks, when a dog, or a child, would suddenly appear from nowhere and frighten him off. Those poor chows spent more time looking around them, checking for unwanted interruptions, than they did looking at the ground, where they needed to be looking! It was all getting a bit much. It was difficult enough finding food without these constant intruders.

Within the chattering there was one special little group of chows. These particular birds were destined for greatness. There were two males, Dirak and Levr, and two females, Bir and Tamig. They weren't related, but had all grown up in the group together, playing hide-and-seek as youngsters among the jagged granite rocks and testing each other's flying skills, just as all chows do. From an early age, Dirak had emerged as the ringleader. He would cheow, "Hey! Look at this huge nest of ants!" and straight away jump up onto a high rock. The other three would rush to the spot where he'd been, and wonder where he'd gone, and what the fuss was about. Then they'd spot Dirak on the rock, and fly up there all at once and push him off, all cheowing excitedly, and soon all four of them would be in the air together, tumbling and swooping, and generally having about as much fun as it was possible for a chow to have. Lots of fun, but at the same time these sort of antics kept them on their toes, and they soon developed into clever young adults. There was something different about them, something that marked them apart from the others.

Since leaving their parents, the four had become inseparable. The other three loved to play tricks on Dirak, who always gave as good as he got. The female Bir was probably the bravest of the four of them. There was the time they spotted a raven who'd been making a nuisance of himself for days, bullying the chows with his friends. This time the raven was out on his own.

"Let's go and have some fun with the bully greatbill!" cheowed Dirak. Within seconds the four daring young chows were up flying alongside the raven, whose friends were nowhere to be found.

"Not so much fun without your friends, eh?!" cheowed Bir to the raven who, of course, couldn't understand a thing. The chows took turns to drop back behind him and then swoop past him at speed, missing him by an inch. The great black bird was becoming quite fearful, making an awful racket. It would be a while before he'd be bullying any chows again. Every time it was Bir's turn to dive-bomb him she'd cut it so fine that she'd actually make contact with the great flapping bird.

"You're crazy! You'll break a wing some day!" cheowed Levr, who was always the one who stopped things getting out of hand. He had as much fun as the rest of them, but his wise head meant that, so far, they hadn't got into more trouble than they could handle. As for little Tamig, well, she didn't like to make a fuss. She went along with everything.

Dirak, Bir, Tamig and Levr joined up with other chows occasionally for a day or two, but always became bored. There was never enough food to go round, so all chows had to work hard getting the most out of a piece of ground, travelling increasing distances in search of their beloved creepy-crawlies. Dirak and his friends of course had to do the same, because they had to eat, but they always managed to find trouble.

One day they went a bit far, and it was crazy Bir's fault as usual. They were foraging with a larger group of around a dozen chows, and Bir spotted a freshly dug rabbit hole. She liked to explore these fully, as they often contained fresh, soft earth so you didn't have to peck your way through the roots of the grass to get to the leatherjackets. Bir pecked and gouged and prised away, getting further and further down the rabbit hole, until she realised she couldn't see anything at all, because it was so dark. At that moment a shaggy brown dog came bounding over the hill towards them all, barking like mad. The chows took off, chewing loud alarm calls as they did. Bir's three friends remained circling over the rabbit hole, but the rest of the group disappeared out of sight. Bir, finally realising something was going on, turned around to see the dog coming right at her. She swiftly turned again, and hopped straight down the hole. For ten minutes the dog stood over the hole, jumping up and down and chasing its tail and sniffing and barking like a deranged thing. The combination of a rabbit hunt and a bird hunt must have been more than the poor creature could bear. Eventually it stopped its frantic activities, sniffed delicately at the rabbit hole, and then trotted off into the distance. Quite some time later Bir burst out of the hole with a loud screech, heading upwards as fast as her wings would take her. If you'd been standing there you'd have had quite a fright. She found her friends who'd been keeping an eye on things from a distance.

"That was close!" she cheowed, not wanting to show that she was actually quite nervous and hadn't known if she'd ever get out of the hole alive.

"You're crazy!" cheowed Dirak the leader, mock-diving her. Actually he was a bit jealous. He wished it had been him. Levr looked across at her and cheowed, sensibly, "At least you got out." After that the chattering realised they were making a nuisance of themselves with their games, so they stayed away from other chows from then on. It would be better for every chow if they carried on on their own. They were grown up, after all. They could look after themselves.

But life was frustrating. Every day was the same story; they'd find themselves flying for ages only to discover that the terrain was completely unsuitable, or there were too many people about, so they'd have to fly back again. They wanted something better. Much better. They simply weren't content foraging all day for the odd few insects in places where the ground was a bit too hard, or the grass was a bit too long, only to return home, still hungry. They observed other birds, and how they behaved. The hundreds of jackdaws they saw every day were having no such problems. They landed constantly on the structures where the big two-legs lived, and even took food from them. They seemed to be taking huge risks in their pursuit of something to eat, but they never went hungry. The gulls were even worse. The chows watched time and again as gulls strolled around amongst the big two-legs. They grabbed at bits of food, and gobbled up all manner of foul-looking things thrown to them by the two-legs. Entirely lacking any kind of dignity or self-respect, but surviving. The chows were repulsed, and yet at the same time they were envious, and wished life could be that easy for them. More than once, the chows landed on a rooftop or a wall, in places where they'd seen the big two-legs. Of course, they made sure there weren't any about beforehand.

"Perhaps we should try going amongst the two-legs," cheowed Tamig desperately one day to Dirak. "Perhaps they've got magic food to give us too!"

"I'm rather afraid it's not a good idea," replied

Dirak, kindly. "I really don't think they've got anything to offer except foul things for the greedy white ones."

"And even the greedy white ones end up flying away in fear," piped up Levr. "For every two-legs that gives them food, there are ten that chase them, or throw things at them. It's too risky!"

"It was just a thought," cheowed Tamig, quietly. Deep down, the chows knew that the people would never be the answer. Hunger was driving them to come up with some odd ideas.

# The Faraway Chow

Constantly at the back of their minds was a story that had been handed down to them by their parents, who had in turn heard it from their parents. It had become known as *The Story of the Faraway Chow*. All four chows knew the story well, for it was the sort of tale that was sure to grab a chow's attention. Dirak's parents, in particular, had told him of the Faraway chow a hundred times, when he was in the nest, when he fledged, and right up to the point when he left them. Their great-great-grandparents had actually known the Faraway chow, it seemed, so they could speak with more authority that other chows. The tale fascinated Dirak.

Several chow generations before, an old, old chow had appeared from nowhere among them. They could see from one look at him that he was no threat because of his age. His feathers were in poor condition, he moved slowly, and was obviously in considerable discomfort, especially when taking off. He was lame in his left leg. The chows couldn't work out why they hadn't seen such an old bird around before. He was a chow all right, just like them, but they could sense that there was also something different about him, something alien. At first he barely made a sound. He was so hungry that he just foraged and foraged to fill his belly. The curiosity mounted as the local chows observed the intriguing stranger. And then finally, after several days, he broke his silence. Sure enough, when he began to communicate, they knew that he must have travelled from far away. His wasn't a different language exactly, but his cheowing had strange inflections and a seductive sort of lilt. It was exotic. It's important to listen to what the old have to say, because they've seen so much more of the world, but this chow was something else entirely. The local chows were mesmerised by the newcomer, and hung on his every utterance.

*"It's wonderful to see you all,"* he began, which pleased the chows very much. *"I have important things to tell."*

He spoke of a land far away, over the great sea, where the sky was once black with chows. He told of terrible things that had happened in the past, stories of things done to the chows that sent awful shivers through their black feathers. But above all he had a message: *"I am the very last chow from that faraway land. I had a mate, but she is long gone,"* he cheowed. *"There are none left there now. Not a single one. But it is our one true home, where all chows belong. When you feel ready, those of you brave enough to make the journey, you must go there. Things will be different. Soon it will be paradise again, and all chows will thrive there, and have everything they need. And they will be loved by all those who see them. I shall not go back, I am too old. I shall die here amongst you, my new friends."*

When they asked him how to find such a place he cheowed, *"It is a long way, over the sea. But a chow can do it easily, if he picks a day when the warm winds are under his wings."* The local chows were enthralled, but confused. The Faraway place sounded terrible, with the old chow's stories about how the food ran out, and how chows were killed for no reason by the two-legs, yet at the same time he was telling them all to go there, because it would be some kind of paradise.

The old Faraway chow disappeared after a few

weeks, but his story stayed with them, and became legend. Over the years, as things became harder for the chows, the legend grew in force, and by the time Dirak and his friends came along it had an almost irresistible pull. There were some nights when they'd roost with empty bellies and the thought of the Faraway chow's promised land on the other side of the sea was all that kept them going. Yet still no chow had made the journey. As Dirak grew older, he became increasingly obsessed with the strange story of the Faraway chow.

And now the cow parsley was in flower, which meant that our four chows were almost two years old. The days were becoming longer and the winter chill was rapidly disappearing. All natural things were embracing the springtime, growing and starting to go about the business of reproducing themselves. All around them, the chows saw other birds nesting and all that that entailed. Some of the chows in the colony had collected material for their nests, even though simply finding enough to eat was a full-time job. Dirak and his three friends looked on, bewildered. It just didn't seem right to be thinking of such things, thinking of bringing more little chows into the world when they lived in a place where there wasn't even enough for the handful who already lived there. They just knew that this wasn't the time.

One evening as the four of them roosted together in their usual spot, Dirak came right out with it: "What about the Faraway chow's promised land? Why don't we go and find it?"

"But it's just a story, just an old tale our parents told us to send us to sleep," replied little Tamig, wide-eyed with fear at the thought.

"Besides, no chow knows exactly where it is," added Levr, ever cautious. But that wasn't the problem. They knew where the Faraway chow's promised land was. All chows knew that if it existed, it was out over the sea. And the sea, well, that was surely no place for a chow, a bird that ate insects from the ground, and roosted on ledges.

# All at Sea

"Well then why don't we at least keep going along the coast? Why do we keep coming back to the same spot to roost, when we have to fly further and further every day looking for food?" cheowed Dirak.

Levr looked concerned. "What are you saying? We try to make a home somewhere else?"

"There must be somewhere with fewer two-legs, and better green stuff. There must be!" Dirak continued, frustrated that the others weren't quite as taken with the idea of a little sea-flying. Bir was keeping quiet. Dirak knew that she would follow him anywhere, because she had a wild spirit. But he was leader, and if half of the group didn't want to fly across the sea, then setting out along the coast seemed like a good compromise. At least they were moving on, which was more than the rest of the colony were prepared to do. They were so much more fed up than the other chows, and all sensed that there must be something better out there, somewhere.

And so, the very next day, the little chattering of four, having made it through another winter, started heading along the coast. The first night they roosted on a ledge on a cliff they'd never been to before, and the feeling was quite exhilarating. The following day they went further still, looking, searching. And as they found themselves flying further and further every day in search of food, they found they liked the feeling. They were nomads. Travellers. Their confidence grew and grew. Even timid Tamig was loving it. Bir didn't seem to be messing about so much any more, because she'd found a purpose. The powerful travelling instinct took over. They loved being on the move, roosting somewhere different every night. With their shared spirit for adventure, the more they travelled, the further they wanted to go.

On the third day they felt unstoppable. They exuded confidence. When they spotted a black-cheeked peregrine cruising low over the cliff tops, they quietly got round behind him and made sure they had the sun behind them before they mobbed him. Although Black-cheeks was faster than any bird in the air, the chows knew that as long as he didn't get a run up, they could easily stay with him and land a few scratches. Bir and Dirak led the attack, and were immediately joined by the other two. They taught him quite a lesson. Black-cheeks squirmed and skewered in the sky, but he couldn't get away unless he simply dived straight down. So the chows made sure they got to him when he wasn't too high; that way he had no escape route. Mobbing Black-cheeks was quite a feeling for a chow, and a good opportunity to convince him that he was much better off attacking lesser birds in the future. A chow, after all, was a very special and clever bird indeed.

On the fourth day, they were continuing along the coastline in the early morning. They dipped and swooped and chased each other, all the while searching for a good spot to land and feed. The air was really starting to warm up now, and the warm breeze felt so good under their wings that they felt they could fly all day just to see where they ended up. They hadn't seen another chow for days. The last time they'd seen one, they'd all given a friendly "Cheeoow!" but didn't even consider stopping. They felt they were on a mission now.

Levr was beginning to wonder where on earth it would end. Dirak couldn't stop thinking about the Faraway chow's promised land. Bir knew it. It seemed that below them there were still never the right places to land. The reality, of course, was that they were looking down on car parks, and hotels, and roads, and villages. But even this would have been all right if there'd still been enough areas of short grass for the chows to forage on. But there weren't.

Just as they approached the brow of a hill they spotted a field up ahead with several ponies in it, and it looked promising. Dirak gave a loud "Cheow!" which meant, "Nice field full of big four legs!" and they flew down low, trying to establish whether the droppings looked old enough to make it worth landing. Just then, a great squadron of gulls appeared out of nowhere, coming over the hill and straight at them. There must have been fifty or more. A terrifying sight, all those great white missiles coming at you, their horrid yellow beaks open, squawking at you to get out of the way. The chows changed direction immediately, but the gulls were doing what they do best, soaring at such a speed that within a second they were among the chows. One of them flew so close to Bir that she thought her time had come. She cheowed with shock and swooped away at the last moment, but as luck would have it, the gull went the same way, giving chase to the annoying chow that had blocked its path. A chow has no trouble keeping its distance from a gull, but it is still a demanding job, requiring all its skill and concentration. Especially when the gull is as angry as this one was. This gull was crazy angry. Needless to say, Bir's friends all joined in the chase, tumbling in the air around the determined gull, bravely dive-bombing it, and generally showing it that it might as well give up and go home. The gull persisted after Bir, who ducked and swooped in every direction, leading the gull a merry dance, and not taking much notice of the direction she was going in. The reality was that she was heading straight out to sea.

Eventually the gull realised it was getting nowhere. All the other gulls were long gone, because of course a gull doesn't stand by its friends like a chow does. So it gave up the chase, peeled away and with a final, defiant squeal headed back the way it had come. Bir now had a chance to check her position. Looking around her, she saw her three best friends in the world, who flew up alongside.

"You think we'd leave you in the lurch?" cheowed Tamig.

They looked down. All they saw was sea. They'd never been out over the sea before, not this far. A chow didn't need to. It felt strange. The world felt bigger, much bigger. The waves they saw below them were more massive than the chows had ever seen. The wind was getting up from the south, and they were familiar with the feeling of the updraughts that were now lifting them. Back home the chows had become experts in riding the warm updraughts that were caused by the wind hitting the cliffs and wafting straight upwards. And now, out to sea, the same thing was happening with the waves. The warm southerly breezes would hit a big wave and be diverted straight upwards where they would meet the underside of the grateful chows. The updraughts weren't quite as dramatic as the ones that would launch a chow vertically upwards when it hopped off a cliff, but there were more of them, and they were exactly what they needed now that they found themselves heading out to sea.

Dirak recognised the opportunity. Up until that moment he'd done the right thing and stayed land-bound. But now fate had stepped in. Thanks to Bir's fight with the gull, they'd found themselves here, and it was simply too good a chance to miss. The blood pounded in Dirak's head. They were hardly having to work at all. It was just too easy. He could think only of one thing; namely the Faraway chow's promised land. He knew the others must be thinking the same thing, but didn't dare call out to them, for fear that it would start up a debate, and they'd all end up deciding to turn back. So he remained silent, only exchanging an occasional "cheow" as a position check. He let Bir go out ahead to make it look less like he was leading them, and he ducked and swooped around her to lighten the mood, and divert the other chows from realising the significance of what they were doing. Never far behind him flew timid Tamig, with sensible Levr, keeping an eye on things at the back.

Thoughts were spinning round Tamig and Levr's heads too, of course. Could this be what they'd been looking for all this time? This was, after all, real adventure. They were flying over the sea! There was no food here, and nowhere to land. It was crazy! It made no sense at all! But it felt as if there was something out there, something better, whether or not it was the Faraway chow's promised land. So they carried on, not looking back. With a southerly tailwind the chows found gliding easy, and if they found themselves losing height, they simply searched for an updraught. They soared on this current of air, hardly flapping their wings at all, just tilting them upwards slightly when necessary to improve their lift. Like carousel horses at the fairground they cut through the air, rising and falling, one calmly taking the lead, then the next, constantly alternating. At one point Tamig cheekily swooped past Bir, catapulting herself way out ahead of the group, before checking herself and resuming her position. "Cheeky thing," muttered Bir to herself.

They were loving this. Ocean-flying was turning out to be much easier than they could have dared hope. The chows were very lucky, really, because if it had been a few days earlier, with a much colder wind coming from the east, there would be a very different story to tell. But animals are never interested in what might have been. They're too busy getting on with it. Before very long they became aware of a hazy, grey strip of something on the distant horizon. It was getting bigger.

"Land!" cheowed Dirak, ecstatically.

"Stormclouds!" Levr replied from the back. In truth, none of them really knew what this distant streak might be, or indeed how far away it was. They'd never actually needed to look at anything this far away before.

"But I can sense it! There's a storm coming, and we're flying right into it!" protested Levr again.

"Well, either way we need to keep going," Bir replied. "We've got no choice now!"

Dirak, Bir and Tamig all continued to set the pace, jostling for the front position, sharing the responsibility. Levr followed. They could see the strip on the horizon growing, and it was starting to look a lot like land.

"See? It *is* land. It *is*!" screeched Tamig, a little overcome.

Then they heard a "Cheow!" from behind. Tamig

glanced back, and realised that the sound had been Levr, cheowing goodbye. He appeared to have turned around and was heading home. The three others stalled in the air and circled, cheowing out to him to stay with the group.

"But it can't be far! Look at the land ahead of us! It *is* land!" cheowed Dirak. He was right, and it now looked closer than the place they'd left behind. But it was still an awfully long way away. Anything could happen. Dirak knew that Levr's flight home against the wind would be ten times harder work. But Levr was determined, and was heading back the way they'd come, struggling determinedly against the gusty wind. Four had become three, and there was nothing they could do about it. That was the last they'd ever see of Levr.

"It's no good," cheowed Dirak, "we just have to keep going! This is no place to dawdle!" They continued on their way.

Everything out here over the sea was different for the chows. They saw so many things they'd never seen before, and some they didn't understand. There were massive pointed objects cutting their way through the surf below them. The chows could see that some of these had big two-legs moving around on them, so they stayed high, out of harm's way. But when they spotted a pod of dolphins racing each other just below the surface of the water, they dropped lower to take a look. Although a dolphin in the water is slower than a chow with the wind behind it, these creatures could still go at quite a pace. Thin, glinting streaks beneath the water's surface, every now and then breaking above it, slicing a clean white foam line. Once in a while one would come right up out of the sea and be a solid, glistening object for one magical instant, before going back down and carrying on the race.

And there were the birds we call gannets, which, until now, the chows had only ever seen from a distance, way out to sea. Now they were flying right over these mighty white birds, and they could see their yellow heads and great black-tipped boomerang wings as they cruised over the high seas, looking out for fish below. This was their domain. These gannets didn't pay any attention to the passing chows. They were too busy. Several times the chows found themselves quite close to a cruising gannet when it would spot something beneath the water. The great bird would drop like a stone, its bill aimed, unwavering, down at its quarry. Then at the very last moment before impact the gannet would fold its wings back and hit the surface like a great white needle, disappearing into the forbidding water below. "Goodness," muttered Tamig to herself, "what a way to go about things."

Now flying, it must be said, is quite the best way to travel. It's just a shame that we people can't manage it without all sorts of contraptions. Flying takes far less energy to travel a far greater distance than, say, running or walking, or any of those boring old ways of getting about. Just watch any bird next time you're near the sea, and you'll see how easy it is for them. Of course, the best thing of all is that nothing gets in your way as it does when you're earth-bound like us. Whoever it was who first said "As the crow flies" meaning "the most direct route possible", really knew what they were talking about. And what a good choice for an expression, using a crow, rather than a pigeon, or a gull! It didn't even take half a day of riding those warm air currents before those three adventurous young chows found themselves approaching land.

What they saw was a different country to the one that they'd come from. Not that that mattered to the chows, because no animal is aware of our silly human boundaries. Dirak couldn't believe they'd made it. He was past caring whether this could really be the Faraway chow's promised land. All the three of them cared about now was whether it was going to be a suitable place to live. They had no idea what the future held, but as they flew over the top of the cliffs and looked down on the rolling landscape of short, short grass, they had a good feeling.

Below them was Yowynk's land.

# Land

One spring afternoon a lady was walking her little white dog along the coast path on the top of the cliffs. She did this walk every day, and loved watching as the landscape changed throughout the year. She revelled in the natural world, and she didn't miss much. The lady had seen a lot of things as she walked the path over the years. Amazing things. She saw rare birds that had been blown off course from far away countries, like the beautiful little crested hoopoe. And she saw others that had stopped off to refuel on their long journey north, like the startling ring ouzel, which you think is just a common blackbird, until it turns around and shows you the white flash across its breast. She'd seen a sunset that burned so red she thought she was dreaming, and been so overpowered by the coconut scent of the furze one summer's day that it had almost knocked her over. She'd lost count of the beautiful adders she'd seen sunning their zigzag backs among the crispy ferns. But despite having seen all these wonders, nothing had prepared her for what she saw this spring day.

Her little white dog had raced ahead along the path, as he normally did, picking up all sorts of scents and sniffing at whatever he could find. The lady saw a patch of wild burnet rose bushes nestling low in amongst the furze, covered in buds. A few of these had already burst open to reveal the first delicate, creamy-white rose flowers, so she bent down and touched one with her nose, closing her eyes and taking in its subtle fragrance. Then, moving on along the path, she looked down at the sea below and was struck by the bright, saffron-gold colour of the lichen, shining in the sun on the wet, black rocks below. What two colours could look nicer together than black and gold, she thought. Possibly only black and red. Then it happened. She knew the sound immediately, but thought she must be hearing things. I mean, they hadn't been seen here for thirty years! In one swift, well-practised movement she raised her binoculars to her eyes and scanned the cliffs for the source of the sound. And there they were, three chows, ducking and swooping along the cliffs in front of her, cheowing to each other as they went. The lady stood there, open-mouthed, and stared. She didn't dare look away, in case they weren't there when she looked back again. Still staring at the chows, she removed her binoculars and blinked in disbelief, then quickly raised them back to her eyes. The chows were still there, chasing each other through the air, skewering and diving, as if they hadn't just flown for half a day non-stop, as if there was simply no other way to fly. Well there wasn't, if you were a chow. After a minute or two the lady accepted what she saw. It was a chattering of chows.

"Welcome home, you three," she muttered, quietly.

Hastily she reached into her coat pocket and retrieved her phone. Glancing at it for no more than a second for fear of losing sight of the birds, she stabbed at the buttons, then pressed it to her ear. "Hello darling. Sorry to call, but I had to," she said, urgently. "Guess what I'm looking at. Choughs. Yes. Choughs. Three of them. They're back".

# The Stinky Cave

It's the adventurous ones that make a difference. These chows were pioneers. They of course had no idea of the effect they were about to have on the human population of Yowynk's land, who'd soon be jumping up and down with excitement. Now that they'd arrived, they simply got on with the business of staying alive, just as any animal would. They were understandably tired after their long and rather unexpected flight. But they were also hungry. They'd set out that morning in search of good new spots to forage, and ended up flying all this way. And all because Bir had got into a scrap with a gull. So they wasted no time landing, and straight away started to forage and peck and fill their hungry bellies.

News travelled fast. People came from miles around to try to catch a glimpse of the new chows. No-one wanted to kill them, or harm them in any way. People only wanted to protect them. There were TV news reports, and they were ecstatic; "They've returned!" they shouted. When people saw them, they had tears in their eyes, and said things like, "I never thought I'd see the day." And the three new chows liked what they were seeing very much. They liked the great long swathes of closely cropped grass, they liked the sight of the animals grazing, and they liked the large rocks that they could forage amongst, and perch and preen on. It felt right. It felt like home.

The Faraway chow had been right. Yowynk's land had changed since he'd left. And there was a good reason. After all those years of watching the last few chows dwindle and then disappear, the people had realised something. They'd worked out that the main reason there were no chows left was because there wasn't enough food for them. All the sheep and cows had been taken from the cliff tops because they were much easier to look after inland in nice neat enclosures, instead of roaming free as they had been before. And with no-one mining any more, they didn't need ponies to carry heavy loads to and from the mines, so they'd all gone from the cliff tops too. With no animals to munch on it, the grass had grown longer and longer. Soon the brambles and furze had started to grow there as well, and it had become impossible for the poor chows to find their lovely creepy-crawlies.

So eventually the clever people who owned the land on the cliff tops had got together, and they'd come up with an idea. They'd agreed to start putting some animals back there to graze. Soon, areas of the cliff tops had started looking much more like they did back in Yowynk's day, with cattle, ponies and sheep grazing happily. Before very long there were lots of places with short, short grass that was springy underfoot. Not the whole coastline, because that would be impossible, but there was quite enough short grass now to provide a choice selection of juicy, crunchy creepy-crawlies for a good number of chows.

Still, although the landscape looked very nice, it hadn't look right without any chows bouncing about on it. So the people had sat back and waited. They'd hoped for the best, crossing their fingers and praying that the chows would return. And now, at last, their prayers had been answered. There were only three of them, but there was a big difference between three and none at all.

A few people didn't understand what all the

fuss was about. "It's just a silly crow with a red beak," they said. But the locals didn't even bother listening. These poor souls didn't understand. The locals knew how important these three chows were. They'd lost them once. They weren't going to let it happen again. Some people even said "Well, these ones don't count because they're foreign! They weren't born here!" But the pioneering chows would soon solve that little problem too.

The three new birds stuck together, feeling quite at home, and saw no reason to ever leave this wonderful place. They came across a nice pointy rock all covered in yellow lichen, with a good flat top on it that caught the sun at midday, perfect for perching and preening. It was under a mighty cliff, and in the middle of the cliff was a dark cave, which could be rather stinky at times, and the cave had a perfect little ledge half way up one wall, just right for a chow to build a nest. And so the following spring the lone female, who we called Tamig, made herself busy whilst the pair we called Dirak and Bir went about the business of building a nest, because the time was right. And they lined it with lots of lovely soft sheep's wool, because there was plenty of it to be found snagged in the hawthorn hedges and the furzey bushes. That clever pair of chows produced a clutch of little speckled eggs, which hatched into three little chow chicks, which grew and grew, and within a few weeks fledged, and before long in Yowynk's land, which we call Cornwall, there was a real, proper chattering of six chows.

So now, if you dress up warm and go out on the cliffs in that beautiful land, where Yowynk hatched in the stinky cave and then was caught in the storm, and where Popet went so hungry, and her brother Codha fell out of the sky, the land where chows died out completely, and then finally came back, and if you keep your eyes open, and your ears too, you may be lucky enough to see a real chow.

Or, of course, hear one!

THE END

# Author's Note

*Shadows in the Sky* is based loosely on the well-documented history of the Cornish chough. Although the adventures described in the book are a fictional interpretation of the story, the events of the three chapters are, I believe, a realistic representation of the Cornish choughs' world in those three centuries: thriving in 1700, dwindling desperately due to persecution and changes in land use by 1900, and returning to Cornwall in 2001, where the birds we called Dirak and Bir began breeding successfully. Whether the very last chough in the Prologue died of old age in Cornwall or, as in the book, flew away to recruit a new generation of choughs is, admittedly, pure conjecture.

There are many vernacular words for chough in Cornwall, including *daw*, *chaw*, *killigrew*, *sea crow* and *chow*. Chow, pronounced as in '*now*', presumably developed historically because it most accurately echoes the bird's cry. In Cornish dialect, the '*ough*' syllable was pronounced as in '*bough*', but in modern English it is more usually pronounced as in '*rough*', so we can see how, as the name was written down, the original Cornish chough (pronounced '*chow*') may have developed into our present day Cornish chough (pronounced '*chuff*').

The chough characters' names are based on the language of their homeland, and are as follows:

Book 1: YOWYNK, 1700

Yowynk (*young* in Cornish).
Lowen (*happy, joyful* in Cornish), Yowynk's sister.
Hogh (*pig* in Cornish), Yowynk's brother.
Cara (*to love* in Cornish), a young chow.

Book 2: POPET, 1900

Popet (*doll* in Cornish).
Codha (*to fall* in Cornish), Popet's brother, known as Sparky to the boy (in Cornish folklore the chough was thought to be a fire starter due to its red bill and feet).
Par (*equal* in Cornish), a chow from the west.

Marthys (*wonderful* in Cornish), Par's sister.

## Book 3: DIRAK AND BIR, 2001

Dirak (*in front of* in Breton).
Bir (*arrow* in Breton), Dirak's mate.
Tamig (*little* in Breton).
Levr (*book* in Breton).